W9-BVL-495

SLEEPING TIGER

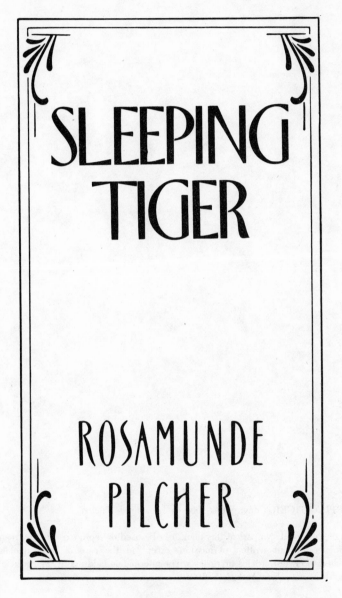

SLEEPING TIGER

ROSAMUNDE PILCHER

St. Martin's Press

The wedding-dress was creamy-white with a suggestion of pink behind it, like the inside of a shell. It was made of very stiff, thin silk, and it swept the red carpet as Selina moved forward, and when she turned, the hem stayed where it was, so that she felt as if the dress were wrapping her up in a luxurious parcel.

Miss Stebbings said, in a high ladylike voice, "Oh, yes, you couldn't choose one prettier than that. It suits you down to the ground." She pronounced it *syuits*. "Now, what about the length?"

"I don't know—what do you think?"

"Let's pin it a little. . . . Mrs. Bellows." Mrs. Bellows moved forward from the corner where she had been standing waiting to be needed. Miss Stebbings wore draped crêpe, but Mrs. Bellows was in a black nylon overall and shoes that

1

looked suspiciously like bedroom slippers. She had a velvet pincushion held to her wrist by a piece of elastic, and knelt down and pinned up a portion of the hem. Selina watched in the mirror. She was not sure if she agreed with Miss Stebbings that the dress *syuited* her down to the ground. It made her look much too thin (surely she had not lost yet more weight!) and the warm colour only emphasised her pallor. Her lipstick had come off and her ears were showing. She tried to shake her hair over her ears and only succeeded in dislodging the small coronet of satin which Miss Stebbings had placed on the top of her head, and when she reached up to push it straight again, she spoiled the set of the skirt, and Mrs. Bellows drew her breath in through her teeth, as though some terrible catastrophe was about to take place.

"Sorry," said Selina.

Miss Stebbings smiled quickly to show it didn't matter, and said conversationally, "And when is the happy day?"

"We thought about a month . . . I think."

"You won't be having a big wedding . . . ?"

"No."

"Of course not . . . under the circumstances."

"I don't really want to have a proper wedding-dress. But Rodney . . . Mr. Ackland . . ." She hesitated again, and then said it: "My fiancé . . ." Miss Stebbings beamed with nauseous sweetness. "He thought I ought to. He said my grandmother would have wanted me to be married in white. . . ."

"Of course she would. How right he is! And I always think a very small, quiet wedding, with the bride in white, has a special charm all of its own. No bridesmaids?"

Selina shook her head.

"Charming. Just the two of you. Finished, Mrs. Bellows? Now. How does that strike you? Just take a step or two." Selina paced obediently. "That's better. We can't have you tripping."

2

Selina wriggled slightly inside the rustling taffeta. "It seems awfully loose."

"I think you're getting thinner," said Miss Stebbings, plucking at the material to make it fit.

"Perhaps I'll get fat again before the wedding."

"I doubt it. Better make a tiny alteration, just to be sure."

Mrs. Bellows hauled herself off her knees and inserted a few pins at the waistline. Selina turned and walked some more, and finally the dress was unzipped, levered delicately off, over her head, and borne away on the arm of Mrs. Bellows.

"When will it be ready?" she asked, pulling her sweater over her head.

"Two weeks, I think," said Miss Stebbings. "And you've decided on this little coronet?"

"Yes, I suppose so. It's quite plain."

"I'll let you have it a few days before, so that you can show it to your hairdresser. It would be rather sweet to have your hair swept up, and through the coronet. . . ."

Selina had an obsession about her ears, which she considered large and ugly, but she said weakly, "Yes," and reached for her skirt.

"And you'll see about the shoes, Miss Bruce?"

"Yes, I'll buy some white ones. Thank you so much, Miss Stebbings."

"Not at all." Miss Stebbings held out the jacket of Selina's suit and helped her into it. She noticed that Selina was wearing her grandmother's pearls, two rows fastened with a sapphire-and-diamond clasp. She noticed, too, the engagement ring, a huge star sapphire, set alternately in pearls and diamonds. She longed to remark on it, but didn't want to be thought inquisitive or vulgar. Instead, in a ladylike silence, she watched Selina pick up her gloves, then held aside the brocade curtain of the fitting-room, and saw her out.

"Good-bye, Miss Bruce. It really has been a pleasure."

"Thank you. Good-bye, Miss Stebbings."

3

* * *

She went downstairs in the lift, walked through various departments, and finally out of the revolving doors and into the street. After the overheated interior of the store, the March day felt nippy. Above, the sky was blue, patterned with racing white clouds, and as Selina moved to the edge of the pavement to call a taxi, the wind caught at her, blew her hair all over her face, her skirt up, dust into her eye.

"Where to?" said the driver, a young man in a sporty checked cap. He looked as though he might race greyhounds in his spare time.

"The Bradley, please."

"Rightey ho!"

The taxi smelt of scented disinfectant with an undertone of stale cigars. Selina got the bit of dust out of her eye, and then rolled down the window. There were daffodils blowing in the park, and a girl on a brown horse, and all the trees were misted with green, the leaves as yet untouched by soot or the dirt of the city. It was not a day for London. It was a day to be in the country, to climb a hill, run down to the sea. The streets and the pavements were crowded with lunch-hour traffic, businessmen, and shopping ladies, and typists, and beatniks and Indians, and lovers, hands entwined, laughing at the wind. A woman sold violets from a barrow by the pavement, and even the old derelict who paced the gutter between a pair of sandwich boards wore a daffodil, perkily, in the lapel of his sagging overcoat.

The taxi turned into Bradley Street, and stopped in front of the hotel. The doorman came to open the door, and let Selina out. He knew her, because he had known her grandmother, old Mrs. Bruce. Selina had been coming to the Bradley for lunch with her grandmother since she was quite a little girl. Now Mrs. Bruce was dead and Selina arrived on her own, but the doorman still knew her, and called her by her name.

"Morning, Miss Bruce."

"Good morning." She opened her bag to find some change.

"It's a lovely day."

"Frightfully windy." She paid the driver, and thanked him, and turned toward the door. "Has Mr. Ackland come yet?"

"Yes, about five minutes ago."

"Oh, bother, I'm late!"

"Doesn't do any harm to keep them waiting."

He spun the door for her, and Selina was injected into the warm, expensive interior of the hotel. There was the smell of fresh cigars, of warm delicious food, of flowers and scent. Elegant little parties of people sat about in groups, and Selina felt windblown and untidy. She was about to sidle in the direction of the Ladies' Room, when the man who sat by himself near the bar saw her, stood up, and came over towards her. He was tall and good-looking, in his middle thirties, dressed in the businessman's uniform of dark grey suit, lightly striped shirt, inoffensive Regimental tie. His face was unlined, well-featured, his ears flat against his head, his brown hair thick and smooth, coming down, at the back, to meet the shining edge of his collar. Across his well-cut waistcoat hung a gold watchchain, and his cuff-links and his watch were also gold. He looked what he was: well-to-do, well-groomed, well-bred, and slightly pompous.

He said, "Selina."

Her flight to the Ladies' abruptly halted, Selina turned and saw him.

"Oh, Rodney . . ."

She hesitated. He kissed her, and said, "You're late."

"I know. I'm sorry. There's so much traffic."

His eyes, though quite kind, conveyed that he thought she looked a mess. She was just about to say, "I must go and powder my nose," when Rodney said, "You go and powder your nose." This, she found maddening. She hesitated for a

5

second, wondering whether to explain that she had been on the point of going to the Ladies' when he had interrupted her, but it hardly seemed worth the trouble. Instead, she smiled, and Rodney smiled back, and, apparently in complete accord, they momentarily parted.

When she returned, her fawn-coloured hair straight and combed, her nose powdered, her lipstick fresh, he was sitting on a small curved satin sofa, waiting for her. In front of him was a small table on which stood his martini and the glass of pale dry sherry which he always ordered for Selina. She went to sit beside him. He said, "Darling, before we talk about anything else, I must tell you this afternoon's off. I've got a client coming to see me at two, rather an important chap. You don't mind, do you? I can make it to-morrow."

Their plan had been to go to the new flat which Rodney had leased, and in which they intended starting their married life. It had recently been re-painted and the plumbing and electrical work was completed, and now all they had to do was to measure and choose carpets, and curtains, and decide on colour schemes.

Selina told him that of course she didn't mind. To-morrow was as convenient as to-day. Secretly, she was grateful for twenty-four hours' grace before she was compelled to make up her mind about the colour of the sitting-room carpet, and the alternative merits of chintz and velvet.

Rodney smiled again, warmed by her acquiescence. He took her hand, moved the engagement ring a little so that the sapphire lay dead centre on her narrow finger, and said:

"And what have you been doing this morning?"

To such a straightforward question Selina had an essentially romantic answer.

"I've been buying my wedding-dress."

"Darling!" He was delighted. "Where did you go?"

She told him. "It sounds very unimaginative, I know, but Miss Stebbings—she's in charge of the model gown department and my grandmother always went there, and I thought I'd rather go to someone I knew. Otherwise I'd probably make the most frightful bloomer and buy something desperate."

"Now why should you do that?"

"Oh, you know how feeble I am with shops; they make me buy anything."

"What's the dress like?"

"Well, it's white, sort of pinky-creamy white. I can't describe it. . . ."

"Long sleeves?"

"Oh, yes."

"And is it short or long?"

Short or long! Selina turned to stare at Rodney. "Short or long? But it's long, of course! Oh, Rodney, do you think I should have got a short one? I never thought of buying a short wedding-dress. I didn't even know you could get them."

"Darling, don't look so worried."

"Perhaps I should have got a short one. As it's going to be such a quiet wedding, a long one's going to look ridiculous, isn't it?"

"You could change it."

"No, I can't. It's being altered."

"Well then . . ." Rodney was soothing. "In that case it doesn't matter."

"You don't think I'll look a fool?"

"Of course not."

"It's very pretty. Really."

"I'm sure it is. And now I have news for you. I spoke to Mr. Arthurstone, and he has agreed to give you away."

"Oh!"

Mr. Arthurstone was Rodney's senior partner, an elderly bachelor, very set in his ways. He suffered from arthritis in his knees, and the thought of coming up the aisle—supporting, rather than being supported by, Mr. Arthurstone—was daunting.

Rodney went on, with raised brows, "Darling, sound a little more pleased than that."

"Oh, I am. It's so nice of him to say he'll do it. But, really, does anybody have to give me away? Can't we just go to the church together, and you and I walk up the aisle and then get married?"

"That really wouldn't do at all."

"But I hardly know Mr. Arthurstone."

"Of course you know him. He's looked after your grandmother's business affairs for years."

"But that isn't the same as knowing him."

"You only have to walk up the aisle with him. Somebody has to give you away."

"I don't see why."

"Darling, this is the way things are conducted. And there is no one else. You know that."

And of course, Selina did know that. No father, no grandfather, no uncle, no brother. Nobody. Only Mr. Arthurstone.

She sighed deeply.

"I suppose so."

Rodney patted her hand again.

"That's my girl! Now, I've got a surprise for you. A present."

"A present?" She was intrigued. Was it possible that Rodney, too, had been affected by the springlike gaiety of this bright March day? Had he, while walking to the Bradley for his lunch date with Selina, been induced into some charming boutique, bought her some useless frivolity to bring a little romance into her day? "Have you, Rodney? Where is it?"

(In his pocket? Expensive presents come in small parcels.)

Rodney reached behind him and produced a package wrapped in stationer's paper and string, which obviously contained a book.

"Here," he said.

Selina tried not to let her disappointment show on her face. It was a book. She hoped that it was a funny one.

"Oh, a book!"

It felt heavy, and hope that it might make her laugh died. It would be an instructive, thought-provoking volume, touching intelligently on various social problems of the day. Or maybe a travel book, with eye-witness accounts of the garish customs of some Central African tribe. Rodney was a great one for improving Selina's mind, and it distressed him deeply that she showed such a marked partiality to magazines, paperbacks and detective stories.

It was the same in other fields of culture. Selina loved the theatre, but could not enjoy a four-hour endurance test about two people living in dustbins. Likewise she was devoted to ballet, but preferred her ballerinas to wear tutus, and waltz to Tchaikovsky, and her musical appreciation did not include solo violin concerts which invariably left her teeth feeling as though she had lately bitten on a sloe.

"Yes," said Rodney, "I've read it myself, but I was so impressed by it that I bought you a copy of your own."

"How very kind." She weighed the parcel up. "What's it about?"

"It's about an island in the Mediterranean."

"That sounds nice."

"It's a sort of autobiography, I suppose. This chap went to live there about six or seven years ago. Converted a house, became very much involved with the local people. His comments on the Spanish way of life struck me as being very balanced, very sane. You'll enjoy it, Selina."

Selina said, "Yes, I'm sure I shall," and laid the parcel down on the sofa beside her. "Thank you very much, Rodney, for buying it for me."

After lunch, they said good-bye on the pavement, standing facing each other, Rodney with his bowler tipped forward

9

over his nose, and Selina carrying the new parcel and with her hair blowing over her face.

He said, "What are you going to do with yourself this afternoon?"

"Oh, I don't know."

"Why not toddle along to Woollands and try to make up your mind about those curtains? If you could get hold of some patterns, we could take them along to the flat when we go tomorrow afternoon."

"Yes." It seemed a sound idea. "That's a good idea."

He smiled at her encouragingly. Selina smiled back. He said, "Well, good-bye then." He did not kiss her in the street.

"Good-bye, Rodney. Thank you for lunch. And the present," she remembered to add.

He made a small gesture with his hand, indicating that neither the lunch nor the present were of any account. Then, with a final smile, he turned and walked away from her, using his umbrella like a walking-stick, and edging swiftly and in a practised fashion between the crowds on the pavement. She waited, half-expecting him to turn for a final wave, but he did not.

Selina, alone, sighed. The day was warmer than ever. All the clouds had been blown away, and she could not bear the thought of sitting in a stuffy shop trying to choose patterns for sitting-room curtains. She walked aimlessly down into Piccadilly, crossed the road, at peril of her life, and turned into the park. The trees were at their prettiest, and grass beginning to be new and green, not brown and dingy with winter any longer. When she walked on the grass it smelt bruised and fresh, like a summer lawn. There were spreading carpets of yellow and purple crocuses, and chairs, in pairs, under the trees.

She went and sat in one of the chairs, leaned back with her legs sprawled and her face turned up to the sun. Soon her skin began to prickle with its warmth. She sat up, and shucked off the jacket of her suit and pushed up the sleeves of her sweater, and thought, I can just as easily go to Woollands tomorrow morning.

A child passed, on a tricycle, with her father walking behind, and a little dog. The child had on red tights and a blue dress and a black band on her hair. The father was quite young, in a polo-necked sweater and a tweed jacket. When the child stopped her tricycle and went over the grass to smell the crocuses he made no attempt to stop her, but watched, holding the tricycle so that it wouldn't roll away, smiling as the little girl bent over, revealing a charming expanse of red tights. The little girl said, "They haven't got a smell."

"I could have told you that," said her father.

"Why haven't they got a smell?"

"I haven't any idea."

"I thought all flowers had a smell."

"Most of them do. Come along now."

"Can I pick them?"

"I shouldn't."

"Why not?"

"The park men don't like it."

"Why not?"

"It's a rule."

"Why?"

"Well, other people like to look at them. Come along now."

The little girl came, clambered back on to her trike and pedalled off down the path, her father behind her.

Selina watched this small scene, torn between pleasure and wistfulness. All her life she had listened in on the lives and conversations of other families, other children, other parents. Their attitudes towards each other caused her endless speculation. As a child, taken to the park by Agnes, her Nanny, she had always hung shyly about at the edge of other people's games, longing to be invited to join in, but too timid to ask. It was not very often that she was invited. Her clothes were always too tidy, and Agnes, sitting knitting on a nearby bench, could look very forbidding. If she thought there was a danger of Selina becoming embroiled with a set of children whom old Mrs. Bruce would obviously consider "unsuitable," then Agnes would roll up her ball of wool, spear it with needles, and announce that it was time to walk back to Queen's Gate.

Here, they were a household of women—a small feminine world, ruled by Mrs. Bruce. Agnes, who had once been her maid, and Mrs. Hopkins, the cook, and Selina, were all her obedient subjects, and a man, unless it was Mr. Arthurstone, Grandmother's lawyer, or, in more recent years, Rodney Ackland, representing Mr. Arthurstone, had scarcely ever entered the house. When one did—to mend a pipe, do a bit of painting, or read the meter—Selina was invariably found in his company, asking questions. Was he married? Did he have children? What were the children called? Where did they go for their holidays? It was one of the few things that made Agnes cross.

"What on earth would your grandmother say if she could hear you at it—keeping the man from his work?"

"I wasn't." On occasions Selina could be stubborn.

"What do you want to talk to *him* for?"

She could not answer because she did not understand why it was so important. But nobody would talk about her father. His name was never mentioned. Selina did not even know what he had been called, for Mrs. Bruce was her mother's mother and Selina had taken her name.

Once, indignant on some score, she had asked outright, "I want to know where my father is. Why haven't I got one? Everybody else has."

She had been told, coldly, but quite kindly, that he was dead.

Selina was taken regularly to Sunday school. "Do you mean he's gone to heaven?"

Mrs. Bruce had tugged at a tiresome knot in her tapestry wool. The idea of That Man consorting with the angels she found hard to swallow, but her religious discipline was strong and it would be wrong to disillusion the child.

"Yes," she said.

"What happened to him?"

"He was killed in the war."

"How killed? How was he killed?" (She could imagine nothing more horrifying than being run over by a bus.)

"We never knew, Selina. We really can't tell you. Now—" Mrs. Bruce glanced at her watch with an air that indicated the conversation was closed. "Go and tell Agnes it's time for your walk."

Agnes, when tackled, proved a little more forthcoming.

"Agnes, my father's dead."

"Yes," said Agnes. "I know."

"How long has he been dead?"

"Since the war. Since nineteen forty-five."

"Did he ever see me?"

"No. He died before you were born."

This was discouraging.

"Did *you* ever see him, Agnes?"

"Yes," said Agnes reluctantly. "When your mother was engaged to him."

"What was his name, Agnes?"

"Now that, I cannot tell you. I promised your grand-mother. She doesn't want you to know."

"Well, was he nice? Was he good-looking? What colour was his hair? How old was he? Did you like him?"

Agnes, who was also highly-principled, answered the one question that she could answer truthfully.

"He was very good-looking. Now, I think that's enough. Hurry along, Selina, and don't drag your feet; you'll scuff the toes of your new shoes."

"I'd like to have a father," said Selina, and later that after-

13

noon spent half-an-hour or more standing watching a father and son sail their model yacht on the Round Pond, edging nearer and nearer all the time in the hope of listening in to their conversation.

She found the photograph when she was fifteen. It was a depressing, wet London Wednesday. There was nothing to do. Agnes had her day off, Mrs. Hopkins was sitting with her arthritic legs on a footstool, immersed in the *People's Friend*. Grandmother had a bridge party. Muted voices and the smell of expensive cigarettes stole from behind the closed drawing-room doors. Nothing to do! Selina, prowling restlessly, came into the spare bedroom, looked at the view from the window, made a few film-star faces into the triple mirror, and was just on the way out when she noticed the books in the small cupboard between the two beds. It occurred to her that she might perhaps find a book she had never read, and with this idea in mind she went to kneel between the beds and run her forefinger along the titles.

It stayed still at *Rebecca*. A yellow-jacketed war-time edition. She took it out and opened it, and a photograph fell from the closely-printed pages. A photograph of a man. Selina picked it up. A man in uniform. Very dark-haired, with a cleft in his chin, his eyebrows irregular, his black eyes glinting with laughter although his face was set in suitable solemn lines. He was a soldier, tailored and well-buttoned, with a glimpse of gleaming Sam Browne across one shoulder.

There was the beginning of a wonderful suspicion. Somewhere, behind the dark amused face, was a suggestion of Selina's own. She took the photograph to the mirror, trying to find resemblances in the planes of her face, the way her hair grew, the squared-off corners of her chin. There wasn't much to go on. He was very handsome, and Selina was plain. His ears lay neatly against his head, and Selina's stuck out like jug-handles.

She turned the photograph over. On the back was written:

Harriet, darling,
from G.

and a couple of crosses for kisses.

Harriet had been her mother's name, and Selina knew then that the photograph was of her father.

She never told anybody about it. She slid *Rebecca* back into the shelf, and took the photograph into her room. After that, she carried it everywhere with her, wrapped in thin paper to keep it clean and crisp. She felt now that she had, at least, a root, however, tenuous, but it still didn't fill her need, and she still watched other families, and still listened in to other people's conversations. . . .

A child's voice penetrated her thoughts. Selina had been dreaming in the sun. Now, awakened, she was aware of the endless roar of Piccadilly traffic, car horns, and the high-pitched chatter of a baby girl, sitting in a push-chair. The other little girl on the tricycle and her father had long since disappeared. Other groups had taken their place, and a loving couple lay, entwined with complete abandon, only a few yards from where Selina sat.

The wooden chair had grown uncomfortable. Selina shifted her position slightly, and the parcel that Rodney had given her slid off her lap and fell on to the grass. Stooping, she picked it up, and aimlessly, without a thought, began to undo it. The dust-jacket of the book was in glossy-white with the lettering in red:

FIESTA AT CALA FUERTE
by George Dyer

15

Selina turned down the corners of her mouth. The book seemed very heavy. She riffled its pages and then closed it, as though she had already finished reading it, with the back of the book lying upwards on her knee.

The face leapt at her, as a name does, suddenly out of a column of newspaper print. It was a casual photograph, blown up to fill the space on the back of the jacket. George Dyer. He wore a white open-necked shirt, and his skin, in contrast, was dark as leather. His face was seamed with lines, they splayed from the corners of his eyes, drew deep channels from nose to mouth, furrowed his brow.

But still, it was the same face. He hadn't changed so much. The cleft was there in the chin. The neat ears, the light in his eye, as though he and the photographer were sharing some outrageous joke.

George Dyer. The author. The man lived on an island in the Mediterranean and wrote about the inhabitants with such balance and sanity. That was his name. George Dyer. Selina picked up her bag, took out the photograph of her father, and, with hands that trembled, held the two photographs alongside each other.

George Dyer. And he had published a book. And he was alive.

2

She took a taxi back to Queen's Gate, ran up the stairs, burst into the flat and called for Agnes.

"I'm here, in the kitchen," Agnes replied.

She was making tea. As Selina appeared in the open kitchen door, Agnes, spooning tea into the pot, looked up. She was a small, ageless person, her slightly sour expression a defence against the tragedies of life, for she had the kindest heart in the world, and she could scarcely bear to hear of hardship or sadness which she was unable to relieve. "Those poor Algerians," she would say, putting on a hat in order to go out and buy a postal order, probably for more than she could afford, and during the Freedom from Hunger campaign she had done without lunch for seven days on end, and suffered cruelly from the resultant tiredness and indigestion.

The lease of the Queen's Gate flat had already been sold,

and when Rodney and Selina were married and moved into their new house, Agnes was going with them. It had taken some time to make her agree to this. Surely Selina wouldn't want old Agnes under her feet . . . she would want a fresh start on her own. Selina had managed to assure Agnes that nothing was further from her mind. Well, Mr. Ackland, then, Agnes argued; heavens, it would be like having his mother-in-law come to live! Rodney, primed by Selina, talked Agnes out of this one. Then she said she didn't like the idea of moving, she was too old to move, so they took her to see the new flat, and she was charmed, as they had known she would be, by the brightness and convenience of it all, the American kitchen filled with sunlight, and the small sitting-room which would be Agnes's own, with a view of the park, and her own telly. After all, she told herself stoutly, she was going with them to help. She was going to work. And, in time, no doubt she would become a Nanny again, with a new nursery to rule, and another generation of babies, an idea that stirred anew all her latent mothering instincts.

Now she said, "You're back early. I thought you were going to go and measure the floors." Selina stood in the door, pink-cheeked from running upstairs, and her blue eyes bright as glass. Agnes frowned. "Is anything wrong, dear?"

Selina stepped forward and laid a book on the scrubbed table between them. She said, looking Agnes straight in the eye, "Have you ever seen that man before?"

Agnes, alarmed, let her gaze slowly drop to the book on the table. Her reaction was more than satisfactory. She gave a small gasp, dropped the caddy spoon, and sat down suddenly on a blue painted chair. Selina half-expected her to place a hand over her heart. She leaned forward across the table. "Have you, Agnes?"

"Oh," said Agnes. "Oh, what a turn you gave me!"

Selina was relentless. "You have seen him before, haven't you?"

"Oh, Selina . . . where did you . . . How did you know
. . . When did you . . ." She was incapable of framing a single question or finishing a single sentence. Selina pulled up a
second chair and sat facing her across the table.

"It's my father, isn't it?" Agnes looked as though she was
about to cry. "Is that his name? George Dyer? Was that my
father's name?"

Agnes pulled herself together. "No," she said. "No, it
wasn't."

Selina looked rebuffed. "Well, what was it?"

"It was Gerry . . . Dawson."

"Gerry Dawson. G. D. The same initials. The same face.
It's a pen-name. It's obvious; it's a pen-name."

"But, Selina . . . your father was killed."

"When?"

"Just after D-day. Just after the invasion of France."

"How do we know he was killed? Was he blown up in
front of an eye-witness? Did he die in somebody's arms? Do
we *know* he's dead?"

Agnes ran her tongue over her lips. "He was missing. Presumed killed."

Hope leapt anew. "Then we don't *know.*"

"We waited three years, and then he was presumed killed.
They let your grandmother know, because Harriet . . . well,
you know. She died when you were born."

"Didn't my father have any family?"

"None that we knew of. That was one of the things your
grandmother objected to. She said he was without background.
Harriet met him at a party; she was never properly introduced,
the way your grandmother would have liked."

"For heaven's sake, Agnes, there was a war on! It had
been going on for five years. Hadn't Grandmother noticed?"

"Well, maybe, but she had her standards and her principles and she stuck by them. There's nothing wrong in that."

"Never mind about it. My mother fell in love with him."

19

"Hopelessly," said Agnes.

"And they got married."

"Without Mrs. Bruce's consent."

"And did she forgive Harriet?"

"Oh, yes, she was never one to hold a grudge. And, anyway, Harriet came back to live here. You see, your father was sent . . . well, in those days they called it Somewhere in England. But he was sent to France . . . on D-Day-plus two, it was. He was killed soon after. We never saw him again."

"So they were married for . . ."

"Three weeks." Agnes swallowed the lump in her throat. "But they had a honeymoon, and they were together for a little while."

"And my mother was pregnant," said Selina. Agnes looked at her in a shocked silence. She still did not expect Selina to use such words, or even to know about such things.

"Well, yes." The face on the back of the dust-jacket caught her eye, and she straightened the book neatly, watching the wicked light in the dark eyes. Brown, they'd been. Gerry Dawson. Was it really Gerry Dawson? It certainly looked like him, or at least the way he would look now if he hadn't been killed, like that, so young and so handsome.

Memories came nudging back and they were not all of them bad. He had given Harriet a glow and a vitality that Agnes had not known she could possess. With Agnes he had flirted mildly, slid her a pound note when nobody was looking. Nothing for Agnes to be proud of to be sure, but it had been a bit of fun, just the same. A bit of fun when life was singularly unfunny. A masculine wind blowing through the house of women. Only Mrs. Bruce had held out against his charm.

"He's a waster," she had announced. "You can tell. Who is he? What is he? Take away the uniform and you're left with a handsome drifter. No sense of responsibility. No thought for the future. What sort of a life can he offer Harriet?"

Of course, in a way, she was jealous. She liked to order

people's lives, to keep a tight rein on the way they behaved, and the money they spent. She had meant to choose, herself, a husband for Harriet. But Gerry Dawson, for all his charm, had a personality and a determination to match her own, and he had won the battle.

Afterwards, after he was dead, after Harriet, not wanting to live, had died, Mrs. Bruce said to Agnes, "I am going to change the baby's name from Dawson to Bruce. I've already spoken to Mr. Arthurstone about it. It seems the obvious thing to do."

Agnes did not agree. But she had never been one to argue with Mrs. Bruce. "Yes, madam," she had said.

"And, Agnes, I would rather she grew up not knowing about her father. It can do her no good, and it might make her feel very insecure. I trust you, Agnes, not to let me down." She held the baby on her knee, and she had raised her eyes, and the two women had watched each other over the fluffy head of the baby.

After a little pause, Agnes had said, again, "Yes, madam," and was rewarded with a brief, cold smile. Mrs. Bruce lifted Selina and placed her in Agnes's arms. "I feel much happier now," she said. "Thank you, Agnes."

Selina said, "You think it's my father, don't you?"

"I don't know for sure, Selina, and that's the truth."

"Why wouldn't you ever tell me what his name was?"

"I promised your grandmother that I wouldn't. Now, I've broken my promise."

"You didn't have any choice."

A thought struck Agnes. "How do you *know* what he looked like?"

"I found a photograph, ages ago. I never told any of you."

"You're not going to do—do anything." Agnes's voice trembled at the very thought.

"I could find him," said Selina.

"What good would it do? Even if it was your father."

"I know it's my father. I just know it is. Everything points that way. Everything you've told me. Everything you've said. . . ."

"If it is, then why didn't he come back to Harriet, after the war?"

"How do we know? Perhaps he was wounded, lost his memory. These things happened, you know." Agnes was silent. "Perhaps my grandmother was so horrid to him . . ."

"No," said Agnes. "That would never have made any difference. Not to Mr. Dawson."

"He'd want to know he had a daughter. That he had me. And I want to know about him. I want to know what he's like and how he talks and what he thinks and does. I want to feel I belong to someone. You don't know how it is, never really belonging to anybody."

But Agnes understood, because she had always known Selina's hunger for what it was. She hesitated and then made the only suggestion she could think of.

"Why don't you talk it over," she said, "with Mr. Ackland?"

The publisher's office was at the top of the building, at the end of an uncertain upward journey by small trembling lifts, short flights of stairs, narrow passages and again, more stairs. Out of breath, and feeling as if she were about to emerge on the roof, Selina found herself in front of a door marked "Mr. A. G. Rutland."

She knocked. There was no reply, only the sound of a typewriter. Selina opened the door and looked in. The girl who was typing glanced up, stopped for a second and said, "Yes?"

"I wanted to see Mr. Rutland."

"Have you an appointment?"

"I called this morning on the telephone. I'm Miss Bruce. He said that if I came about half past ten . . ." She looked at the clock. It was twenty past. The typist said, "Well, he's got someone in with him now. You'd better sit down and wait."

She went on typing. Selina came into the room, shut the door and sat down on a small, hard chair. From the inner office came the murmur of male voices. After twenty minutes or so, the murmur became more animated, and there was the sound of a chair being pushed back, and footsteps. The door to the inner office opened, a man came out, pulling on his overcoat and dropping a folder of papers.

"Oh, careless of me. . . ." He stooped to scoop them up. "Thank you, Mr. Rutland, for everything. . . ."

"Not at all; come back when you've got some fresh ideas about the dénouement."

"Yes, of course."

They said good-bye. The publisher began to return to his office, and Selina had to stand up and say his name. He turned and looked at her.

"Yes?" He was older than she had imagined, very bald, with the sort of spectacles you can either look through or over. He was looking over them now, like an old-fashioned schoolmaster.

"I . . . I think I have an appointment."

"You do?"

"Yes. I'm Selina Bruce. I called this morning."

"I am very busy . . ."

"It won't take more than five minutes."

"Are you a writer?"

"No, it's nothing like that. I just wanted you to help me . . . to answer some questions."

He sighed. "Oh, very well."

He stood aside and let Selina walk past him and into his office. There was a turkey-red carpet and a littered desk, and shelves and shelves of books, and books and manuscripts piled on the tables, and on the chairs and even on the floor.

He did not apologise for any of this. He obviously saw no

23

need . . . and indeed there was none. He pushed forward a chair for Selina and went to settle himself behind his desk. Before he was even thus installed, she had begun to explain.

"Mr. Rutland, I really am sorry to bother you and I won't take a moment more than I have to. But it's about that book you published, *Fiesta at Cala Fuerte.*"

"Oh, yes. George Dyer."

"Yes. Do—do you know anything about him?"

This blurted question was met with an unnerving silence and an even more unnerving glance over the top of Mr. Rutland's spectacles.

"Why?" said Mr. Rutland at last. "Do you?"

"Yes. At least I think I do. He was a . . . friend of my grandmother's. She died about six weeks ago, and I . . . well, I wanted to be able to let him know."

"I can always forward a letter for you."

Selina took a deep breath and proceeded to attack on another flank.

"Do you know very much about him?"

"I should think as much as you. I presume you've read the book."

"I mean . . . you've never met him?"

"No," said Mr. Rutland, "I haven't. He lives at Cala Fuerte on the island of San Antonio. He has lived there, I believe, for the last six or seven years."

"He never came to London? Even for the publication of the book?" Mr. Rutland shook his bald head so that the light from the window gleamed upon it. "Do . . . do you know if he's married?"

"He wasn't at the time. He may be by now."

"And how old is he?"

"I haven't any idea how old he is." He began to sound a little impatient. "My dear young lady, this is wasting my time."

"I know. I am sorry, I just thought you could help me. I

24

thought there was the chance that he might have been in London, now, and I could have seen him."

"No, I'm afraid not." Firmly, Mr. Rutland stood up, indicating that the interview was over. Selina stood up too, and he went to the door and opened it for her. "But if you do want to get in touch, we will be pleased to forward any correspondence on to Mr. Dyer."

"Thank you. I'm sorry to have wasted your time."

"Not at all. Good morning."

"Good-bye."

But as she went through the door and crossed the outer office, she looked so despondent that Mr. Rutland's heart, despite himself, was touched. He frowned a little, removed his glasses, and said, "Miss Bruce."

Selina turned.

"We send all his letters to the Yacht Club in San Antonio, but his house is called the Casa Barco, Cala Fuerte. It might save time if you wrote to him direct. And if you are writing, remind him that I'm still waiting for the synopsis of that second book. I've written him a dozen letters, but he seems to have a built-in aversion to answering them."

Selina smiled, and the publisher was amazed at the transformation it wrought to her whole appearance. She said, "Oh, thank you. I am grateful."

"Not at all," said Mr. Rutland.

The empty flat was not the most suitable place for a discussion of such importance, but there was no other.

Selina cut short Rodney's observations on the relative merits of plain and patterned carpets, and said, "Rodney, I must talk to you."

Interrupted, he looked down at her in mild annoyance. He had though, all through lunch, and the subsequent taxi ride, that she did not seem herself. She had eaten scarcely anything, and had seemed preoccupied and vague. Furthermore, she was wearing a blouse which did not seem to go with her fawn coat and skirt, and he had spied a ladder in her right stocking. Selina was normally as well-groomed and co-ordinated as a Siamese cat, and these small irregularities worried him.

He said, "Is anything wrong?"

Selina tried to meet his eye, to take a deep breath and be entirely calm, but her heart was thumping like a sledge-hammer, and her stomach felt as though she had just ascended in a too-fast lift, leaving most of her innards in the basement.

"No, there's nothing wrong, but I simply have to talk to you."

He frowned. "Won't it keep till this evening? This is the only chance we'll get to measure the . . ."

"Oh, Rodney, please help me and listen."

He hesitated, and then with a resigned expression, laid down the book of carpet samples and folded his foot-rule and slid it into his pocket.

"Well? I'm listening."

Selina licked her lips. The empty flat unnerved her. Their voices echoed, and there was no furniture, and no ornament with which to fiddle, no cushion to plump into shape. She felt as if she had been put on to a large, empty stage, with no props and no cues, and she had forgotten her lines.

She took a deep breath and said, "It's about my father."

Rodney's expression scarcely changed. He was a good lawyer, and he enjoyed a game of poker. He knew all about Gerry Dawson, for Mrs. Bruce and Mr. Arthurstone had long since deemed it necessary to keep him informed on such facts. And he knew that Selina didn't know anything about her father. And he knew that he was not going to be the one to tell her.

"What about your father?" he said, quite kindly.

"Well . . . I think he's alive."

In relief, Rodney took his hands out of his pockets and gave a small snort of incredulous laughter. "Selina. . . ."

"No, don't say it. Don't say he's dead. Just listen, for a moment. You know that book you gave me yesterday? *Fiesta at Cala Fuerte*. And you know it had on the back a photograph of the author, George Dyer?"

Rodney nodded.

"Well, the thing is . . . he looks exactly like my father."

Rodney digested this, and then said, "How do you know what your father looked like?"

"I know, because I found a photograph of him, ages ago, in a book. And I think it's the same person."

"You mean George Dyer is . . ." He stopped just in time.

"Gerry Dawson," Selina finished, triumphantly, for him.

Rodney began to feel as if a carpet was being pulled from beneath his feet.

"How did you know his name? You were never meant to know his name."

"Agnes told me yesterday."

"But, Agnes has no business . . ."

"Oh, Rodney, try to understand! You can't blame her. I caught her unawares. I put the face of George Dyer like *that*, flat down on the table in front of her, and she practically fainted away."

"Selina, you do realise that your father is dead?"

"But Rodney, don't you see, he was missing? Missing, presumed killed. Anything might have happened."

"Then why didn't he come back after the war?"

"Perhaps he was ill. Perhaps he lost his memory. Perhaps he heard that my mother had died."

"And what's he been doing all this time?"

"I don't know. But for the last six years he's been living on San Antonio." She realised that Rodney was going to ask her how she had found that out, and she added quickly, "It

27

tells you all about this in his book," because she didn't want him to know that she had been to see Mr. Rutland.

"Have you got the photograph of your father with you?"

"Not the book one."

"I didn't mean that. I meant the other."

Selina hesitated. "Yes, I have."

"Let me see it."

"You'll . . . give it back . . . ?"

A slight tinge of irritation crept into Rodney's voice. "My dear child, what do you take me for?"

She was immediately ashamed, for Rodney would never stoop to an underhand action. She went for her bag, took out the precious photograph, and handed it across the Rodney. He carried it to the light of the window and Selina followed to stand beside him.

"You probably won't remember the photograph on the back of the book, but it is the same person, I'd swear to it. Everything is the same. The cleft in the chin. And the eyes . . . and the way the ears are set."

"What did Agnes say?"

"She wouldn't commit herself, but I'm sure she thinks it's my father."

Rodney did not reply. Frowning down at the dark, amused face in the photograph he was visited by a number of anxieties. The first was the possibility of losing Selina. A painfully honest man, Rodney had never deluded himself that he was in love with her, but she had become, almost without his realising it, a pleasant part of his life. Her appearance, with her satin, fawn-colored hair and skin and her sapphire-blue eyes, he found beguiling, and although her interests were not perhaps as esoteric as Rodney's own, she showed a charming willingness to learn.

And then, there was the question of her business affairs. Since her grandmother's death Selina was a girl of some property, a ripe fruit, if ever there was one, to fall into the hands of a possibly unscrupulous man. At the moment, Rodney and Mr. Arthurstone, in complete accord, were handling her stocks and trusts, and in another six months Selina would be twenty-one, and after that any final decisions would be her own. The thought of the control of all that money passing out of his hands gave Rodney the shivers.

He looked down, over his shoulder, and met Selina's eyes. He had never known any girl with such blue whites to her eyes. Like detergent advertisements. She smelt vaguely of fresh lemons . . . verbena. Out of the past he seemed to hear Mrs. Bruce's voice, and some of the biting things she had had to say about Gerry Dawson. *Shiftless* was the word that stuck in Rodney's mind. Further epithets presented themselves to him. Irresponsible. Unreliable. Financially unsound.

He held the photograph by the corner and tapped it into the palm of his left hand. He said, at last, in a small burst of annoyance, finding it necessary to blame somebody for the situation in which he found himself, "Of course, it's all your grandmother's fault. She should never have kept you in the dark about your father. This web of secrecy, never mentioning his name . . . was a ridiculous mistake."

"Why?" asked Selina, interested.

"Because it's given you an obsession about him!" Rodney shot at her. Selina stared, obviously deeply hurt, her mouth hanging slightly open like an astounded child's. Rodney plunged ruthlessly on.

"You have an obsession about fathers, and families and family life in general. The fact that you found this photograph, and kept it—hidden—is a typical symptom."

"You talk as if I had measles."

"I'm trying to make you understand that you have a complex about your dead father."

"Perhaps he isn't dead," said Selina. "And if I have got a complex about him, you've just admitted that it isn't my fault.

29

ROSAMUNDE PILCHER

What's so wrong about having a complex? It isn't like a squint, or a wall eye. It doesn't show."

"Selina, this isn't funny."

"I don't think it's funny either."

She was regarding him with a bright gaze that he told himself could be described as a glare. They were quarreling. They had never quarrelled, and this was surely not the time to start. He said, quickly, "Darling, I'm sorry," and bent to kiss her mouth, but she turned her face aside and he caught her cheek. "Don't you see, I'm only thinking of you. I don't want you to get caught up with some man, go chasing him to the ends of the earth, and then find you've made a foolish mistake."

"But, supposing," said Selina, "just supposing it really *was* my father. Alive, and living in San Antonio. Writing books and sailing his little yacht and making friends with all the local Spanish people. You'd want me to get to know him, wouldn't you? You'd want to have a proper father-in-law of your own."

It was the very last thing Rodney wanted. He said gently, "We mustn't just think of ourselves. We must consider him, too —George Dyer—whether he's your father or not."

"I don't understand."

"By now, after all these years, he's made a fine life for himself. It's a life he chose of his own free will. If he'd wanted a family and the ties of a wife and sons . . . and daughters . . . he'd have got them for himself by now. . . ."

"You mean he wouldn't want me? He wouldn't want me to go and find him?"

Rodney was shocked. "You aren't considering such a step?"

"It's so important to me. We could fly to San Antonio."

"We?"

"I want you to come with me. Please."

"It's out of the question. Besides I have to go to Bournemouth, I told you, and I'll be away for three or four days."

30

"Can't Mrs. Westman wait?"

"Of course she can't wait."

"It's just that I want you to be with me. Help me, Rodney."

Rodney misunderstood this plea. He thought she meant "Help me" in the practical sense. Help me buy an air ticket, help me get to the right aeroplane, help me through the customs, find me the taxis and the porters. She had never travelled any distance on her own in her life, and he was quietly confident that now she would never try.

He parried her plea with a small spurt of charm, smiled, and took her hand and said, placatingly, "Now, what's all this rush about? Be patient. I know this must be exciting for you, to suddenly suspect that your father is alive. I realise, too, that there's always been something of a void in your life. I hoped I was going to be able to fill it."

He sounded noble. Selina said, "It isn't that, Rodney. . . ."

"But, you see, we don't know anything about George Dyer. Oughtn't we to make a few quiet investigations before we take any steps we might regret?" He was talking like Royalty.

"I was born after he was reported missing. He doesn't even know I exist."

"Exactly!" Rodney risked a more forceful tone. "You know, Selina, there's an old saying and a very true one: Never wake a sleeping tiger."

"I don't think of him as a tiger. I just think about maybe he's alive and he's the one person I've wanted, more than anybody, all my life."

Rodney vacillated between being offended and being angry.

"You're talking like a child."

"It's like a penny. A penny's got two sides, heads and tails. I have two sides as well. A Bruce side and a Dawson side.

31

Selina Dawson. That's what I'm really called. That's who I really am." She smiled at Rodney, and he thought, in his distress, that it was a smile he had never seen before. "Do you love Selina Dawson as much as you love Selina Bruce?" He was still holding the photograph of her father. She took it from him and went to return it to her bag.

Rodney said, only a little late on cue, "Yes, of course I do."

Selina closed her bag, and laid it down. "Now," she said, smoothing down the front of her skirt as though she were about to start a recitation, "isn't it time we measured this floor?"

3

Barcelona Airport, in the first pale light of dawn, was deep in puddles from the storm which had chased the aircraft across the Pyrenees. There was a thin wind, blowing down from the mountains, the airport officials all smelt of garlic, and in the lounge the benches and chairs were sunk with still-sleeping figures, tumbled in coats and rugs, bag-eyed and blue-chinned from hours of waiting. It had been a bad night. Flights from Rome and Palma had been cancelled. Flights from Madrid were late.

Selina, still queasy from her flight, came in through the swinging plate-glass doors, and wondered what to do next. She had a through ticket to San Antonio, but needed another boarding pass. At a counter a tired-looking official was weighing some luggage, so she went and stood hopefully in front of him, and presently he looked up and she said, "Do you speak English?"

"Sí."

"I have a ticket for San Antonio."

Without expression, he held out a hand for it, ripped the relevant page from the ticket book, made out a boarding pass, slid the pass back into the ticket, and returned it to her.

"Thank you. What time does the plane go?"

"Half past seven."

"And my luggage?"

"It is marked through to San Antonio."

"And the Customs?"

"Customs at San Antonio."

"I see. Thank you so much." But her ingratiating efforts to raise a smile were not successful. The man had had a hard night and he was in no mood to be pleasant.

She went and sat down. She ached with exhaustion, but she was too nervous to feel sleepy. The plane had left London Airport at two in the morning, and she had sat staring into darkness and telling herself briskly to take things one at a time. Barcelona. San Antonio. Customs and passports and things. Then a taxi. It would be quite easy to find a taxi. And then Cala Fuerte. Cala Fuerte would not be large. Where does the Englishman, George Dyer, live? she would ask, and they would be able to direct her to the Casa Barco, and there she would find him.

The storm hit them as they came over the Pyrenees. The captain had had warning of it, and they were all woken and buckled into their safety belts. The plane lurched and wobbled, climbed higher and lurched some more. Some passengers were sick. Selina, closing her eyes, willed herself not to be, but it had been a close shave.

As they came down into Barcelona, the lightning attacked them, seeming to fly like banners from the wing tips. Once through the clouds they were lashed by rain, and when they landed at Barcelona, rocketing down through a cross wind, the runway was waterlogged, and shimmering with reflected lights. As the wheels brushed the tarmac, they sent up great wings of water, and there was an audible sigh of relief from everybody when at last the plane trundled to a standstill and the engines were stilled.

It was strange not having anyone to meet her. There should be a driver, a chauffeur in a uniform, with a large warm car. Or Agnes, fussing with rugs. There should be someone to find her suitcase, and deal with officialdom. But there was no one. This was Spain; Barcelona at six o'clock on a March morning, and there was no one but Selina.

When the hands of the clock had crept round to seven o'clock, she went into the bar and bought a cup of coffee, paying for it with some pesetas that the thoughtful man in the bank had insisted she bring with her. It was not very good coffee, but comfortingly hot, and she sat drinking it and watching her own reflection in the mirror that backed the bar. She wore a brown jersey dress and a coat the colour of porridge, and a silk headscarf, slipping now off the back of her hair. *Travelling-clothes* Mrs. Bruce called them. She had set ideas about travelling-clothes. Jersey is comfortable and doesn't crease, and the coat must go over everything. Shoes must be light, but sturdy enough for long walks over windswept airports, the handbag large and capacious. Automatically, even in moments of drama, Selina followed this excellent and unvarying advice. Not that it helped. She still looked a mess and felt exhausted. She was afraid of flying, and dressing like a knowledgeable traveller didn't make you one, nor dispel the conviction that you would either die in an air crash or lose your passport.

The plane to San Antonio seemed very small, and looked as unreliable as a toy. Oh, no, thought Selina as she walked out towards it, with the wind blowing gusts of petrol fumes into her face and the puddles splashing over the tops of her shoes. There were only a few passengers and they filed glumly into the aircraft as though they shared her convictions. Once strapped in, Selina was given a glucose sweet, and began to eat it as though it were a new miracle cure for sheer funk. It wasn't, but the plane did not crash.

The bad weather, however, was still about, and they did not see San Antonio until they came in to land. There was nothing but cloud, lumps of grey cotton wool at the windows. Then there was rain, and then, unexpectedly, fields and the tops of houses and a windmill and a bunch of pines and earth the colour of brick, and everything glistening in the rain. The airport had only just been built, the landing-strip bulldozed out of the soil, and now the runway was a sea of red mud. After they had landed, two mechanics manhandled a gangway up to the side of the aircraft. They wore yellow slickers and were spattered in mud up to their knees. For once nobody seemed over-anxious to leave the aircraft. When they did, they went cautiously, picking their way between the puddles.

San Antonio smelled of pines. Wet, resinous pines. The rain, miraculously, seemed to have stopped. It was warmer, with no bite to the wind. There were no snow-topped mountains here, only the warm, surrounding sea. This was San Antonio. The flying was over and she was still alive. Selina pulled off her headscarf and let her hair blow in the wind.

There was a queue for immigration. Members of the Guardia Civil stood about as though they were expecting an influx of criminals. They wore guns, and not for ornamental reasons. The immigration official worked slowly. He was holding a conversation with a colleague. It was long and involved, an argument of sorts, and he only stopped short at intervals in order to inspect painstakingly, page by page, any alien passport. Selina was the third and she had been waiting ten minutes before he eventually stamped "ENTRÀDA," and handed it back to her.

She said tentatively, "My luggage . . . ?"

He did not understand, or did not want to, but waved her on. She put her passport back into her sensible bag, and went on searching on her own. For a small airport, San Antonio in the early morning seemed unusually crowded, but at nine-thirty the Barcelona plane returned to Spain, and this was a popular flight. Families gathered, children cried, mothers entreated them loudly to stop. Fathers argued with porters, queued for tickets and boarding passes. Lovers stood about hand-in-hand, waiting to say good-bye, and getting in everybody's way. The noise, in the high-ceilinged building, was deafening.

"Excuse me," Selina kept saying, trying to work her way through the throng. "I am sorry . . . excuse me . . ." Some of her fellow-passengers were already gathered beneath a sign which said "ADUANA," and she struggled to join them. "I am sorry"—she tripped over a bulging basket, and nearly knocked down a fat baby in a knitted yellow coat. "Excuse me, please."

The luggage was already arriving, manhandled on to the makeshift counter, claimed, examined, sometimes opened, finally passed by the Customs officer, and removed.

Selina's suitcase never appeared. It was a blue one with a white stripe and easy to identify, and after an eternity of waiting she realised that there was no more luggage to come, the other passengers had, one by one, filtered away, and Selina was alone.

The Customs officer, who had, up to now, successfully managed to ignore her, hitched hands on his hips and raised his black eyebrows at her.

"My suitcase . . ." Selina said. "It's . . ."

"No hablo Inglese."

"My suitcase . . . Do you speak English?"

A second man moved forward. "He says 'No.' "

"Can you speak English?"

He shrugged elaborately, suggesting that maybe, under

37

desperate circumstances, he might possibly manage a word or two.

"My case. My luggage." She broke desperately into French. "*Mon bagage.*"

"Not here?"

"No."

"Where you come from?" He rolled all his r's with a great flourish. "Wherre you come frrom?"

"Barcelona. And London."

"Oh!" He made it sound as though she had imparted grave news. He turned to his colleague and they began to speak, a liquid rattle of Spanish that might have been a private conversation. Selina wondered desperately if they were exchanging family news. Then the English-speaking man shrugged again, and turned back to Selina. "I will find out," he said.

He disappeared. Selina waited. The first man began to pick his teeth. Somewhere a child wailed. The loudspeaker, to add to the misery, burst into the sort of music normally associated with bullfights. After ten minutes or more the helpful man came back, with one of the stewards from the aircraft.

The steward said, smiling as though he were imparting a charming favour, "Your suitcase is lost."

"*Lost!*" It was a despairing wail.

"Your case is, we think, in Madrid."

"*Madrid!* What's it doing in Madrid?"

"Unfortunately, at Barcelona, it has been put on the wrong truck . . . we think. At Barcelona there is also a plane going to Madrid. We think that your luggage is in Madrid."

"But it was labelled to San Antonio. It was labelled in London."

At the word "London" the Customs man made his hopeless sound again. Selina felt she could hit him.

"I am sorry," said the steward. "I will have a message sent through to Madrid, to return the case to San Antonio."

"How long will that take?"

"I did not say it was in Madrid," said the steward, determined not to commit himself. "We must find out."

"Well, how long will it take to find out?"

"I do not know. Maybe three, four hours."

Three or four hours! If she was not angry, then she would cry. "I can't wait here three or four hours."

"Then perrhaps you can come back. To-morrow, maybe, to see if the suitcase is here. From Madrid."

"But can't I call you? Ring you? On the telephone?"

This was apparently a joke. Through smiles, she was told, "Señorita, there are few telephones."

"Then I have to come back here to-morrow, to see if you have found my case?"

"Or the next day," said the steward, with the air of a man full of bright ideas.

Selina made a final appeal. "But everything I have is in my case."

"I am sorry."

He continued to stand smiling at her. She felt at that moment as though she were drowning. She looked from one face to another, and slowly realised that nobody was going to help her. Nobody could help her. She was alone and she had to help herself. She said at last in a voice that shook only a little, "Is it possible for me to find a taxi?"

"But of course. Outside. There are many taxis."

There were, in fact, four. Beginning to be oppressed by the warmth of the porridge-coloured travelling-coat, Selina went in search of them. As soon as she appeared, the drivers all blew their horns, waved, called "Señorita," leapt from their cars and rushed for her custom, each trying to channel Selina towards his own vehicle.

She said, loudly, "Can any of you speak English?"

"*Sí. Sí. Sí.*"

"I want to go to Cala Fuerte."

"Cala Fuerte, *sí.*"

"Do you know Cala Fuerte?"

"*Sí. Sí,*" they all said.

"Oh, can't anybody speak English . . . ?"

"Yes," said a voice. "I can."

It was the driver of the fourth taxi. While his colleagues had tried to beguile Selina, he waited, placidly finishing his cigar. Now he dropped the odorous stub, stepped on it, and moved forward. His appearance was not reassuring. He was an enormous man, very tall and equally fat. He wore a blue shirt, open-necked and revealing a black, furry chest. His trousers were slung by an intricately worked leather belt, and on the back of his head was an incongruous straw hat, of the variety that tourists bring back from holiday. He wore, at this early, cloudy hour, sunglasses, and narrow black moustaches suggesting unknown Don Juan qualities. He looked so villainous that Selina reeled.

"I speak English," he said, with a strong American accent. "I work in Spain, on a U.S. Army air base. I speak English."

"Oh. Well . . ." Surely any of the other three taxi-drivers was preferable to this ruffian, English or not!

He ignored her hesitation. "Where d'you want to go?"

"To . . . Cala Fuerte. But I'm sure . . ."

"I'll take you. Six hundred pesetas."

"Oh. Well . . ." She looked hopefully at the other taxi-drivers, but already they seemed discouraged. One had even returned to his car and was rubbing on the windscreen with an old rag.

She turned back to the large man in the straw hat. He smiled, a broken-toothed leer. She swallowed, and said, "All right. Six hundred pesetas."

"Where is your luggage?"

"It is lost. It was lost in Barcelona."

"That's bad."

"Yes, it got put on the wrong plane. They're going to find

out, and I'll get it to-morrow or the next day. I have to go to
Cala Fuerte now, you see, and . . ."

Something in the big man's expression made her stop. He
was gazing down at Selina's handbag. Selina followed his gaze,
and saw that, indeed, something strange had happened. Although the two sturdy straps were still over her arm, the bag
hung open like a gaping mouth. The front straps had been
neatly cut, as if with a razor blade. And her wallet was missing!

The taxi-driver was called Toni. He introduced himself
formally, and then he acted as her interpreter during the long
and tedious interview with the Guardia Civil.

*Yes, the señorita had been robbed. In the crowd at the
airport this morning, had been a thief with a razor blade. She
had been robbed of everything. Everything she owned.*

Her passport?

*Not her passport. But her money, her pesetas, her British
money, her traveller's cheques, her return ticket to London.*

The Guardia Civil, with concentration, examined Selina's
bag.

Had the Señorita felt nothing?

*But nothing. Pushing through the crowds, how could she
feel anything?*

The bag looked as if it had been cut by a razor.

That was it. A razor. A thief with a razor blade.

What was the Señorita's name?

*It was Miss Selina Bruce, of London, travelling on a Brit-
ish passport.*

*And where was Miss Bruce's place of residence, in San
Antonio?*

It was . . . Selina hesitated here, but events had gone
beyond hesitation. *Casa Barco, Cala Fuerte.*

*What colour was the wallet? How much money, exactly?
Were the traveller's cheques signed?*

Wearily she answered the questions. The clock crawled
round to ten, to half past ten and beyond. The worst of her

41

apprehensions had more than been fulfilled. She had lost her suitcase and she had lost her money. And she still had to get to Cala Fuerte.

At last it was over. The Guardia Civil squared off his papers and stood up. Selina thanked him, and shook hands. He looked surprised, but still did not smile.

Together, Selina and Toni crossed the now empty airport building, went out through the glass doors, and stopped, facing each other. Selina held her coat over her arm, for it had begun to get uncomfortably warm, and watched him, waiting for him to make the first move.

He took off his dark glasses.

She said, "I still have to get to Cala Fuerte."

"You have no money."

"But you'll get paid, I promise you. When we get to Cala Fuerte . . . my . . . father will pay your fare."

Toni frowned enormously. "Your father? You have a father here? Why didn't you say?"

"It wouldn't have made any difference. We . . . we couldn't get in touch with him. Could we?"

"Your father *lives* in Cala Fuerte?"

"Yes. At a house called the Casa Barco. I am sure he will be there, and will pay you." Toni watched her, suspicious and unbelieving. "And you can't just leave me here. I haven't even got my plane ticket back to London."

He stared into space for a bit, then decided to light a cigarette. He was giving nothing away, and refusing to commit himself.

"You said you'd take me," Selina went on. "And I'll see that you're paid. I promise."

His cigarette was lighted. He blew a cloud of smoke into the air, and his black eyes swivelled back to Selina's face. She looked anxious and pale, but also, undoubtedly, well-to-do. The ruined handbag was alligator, and the good shoes matched. The scarf was silk, and both the dress and the coat of

42

expensive wool. Sometimes, as she moved, Toni glimpsed the gold of a thin chain around her neck, and she wore a gold watch. There was, undoubtedly, money around—if not in the handbag, then somewhere. It was only March and there were not yet so many taxi fares that he could afford to turn down a good one. And this girl, this young *Inglesa*, did not look capable of tricking anybody.

He made up his mind. "All right," he said at last. "We go."

4

~~~~

Made beneficent by his own kindness, Toni talked expansively.

"San Antonio, until five years ago, was a very poor island. The communications with Spain were lousy, only a small boat twice a week. But now we have the airport, so that visitors come and in the summer there are a lot of people, and things are getting O.K."

Selina thought that the first thing that needed to get O.K. was the surface of the roads. The one they were on was unsurfaced and rutted with car tracks, on which the aged Oldsmobile, which was Toni's taxi, rocked and bucketed like a ship at sea. It wound, between low, dry-stone walls, through a countryside squared off into little farmsteads. The ground looked stony and unpromising, the squat buildings had been bleached by the fierce sun to the colour of pale sand. The

women, who worked in the fields, wore black skirts to their
ankles and black scarves about their heads. The men were in
faded blue, ploughing the unresponsive earth, or jolting, in
wooden carts, behind a pair of mules. There were flocks of
goats, and scrawny chickens, and every mile or so a well, cir-
cled by a patient, blinkered horse, and a water-wheel, spilling
brimming buckets into the irrigation ditches.

Selina noticed this, and said, "But you had rain last
night."

"That was the first rain for months. We are always short of
water. There are no rivers, only springs. The sun is already
hot, and the ground dries very fast."

"We flew through a storm last night, over the Pyrenees."

"The bad weather has been in the Mediterranean for
days."

"Is it always like this in March?"

"No, it can be warm in March." And, as if to substantiate
his words the sun, at that moment, chose to filter through a
gap in the clouds and paint everything in a thin golden light.
"Over there," Toni went on, "that is the town of San Antonio.
The cathedral on the top of the hill is very old, a fortified
cathedral."

"Fortified?"

"Against attack. From the Phoenicians, and Pirates, and
Moors. For centuries the Moors occupied San Antonio."

The town lay like a frieze against the back-drop of the sea.
A hill of white houses, topped by the soaring towers and spires
of the cathedral.

"We're not going through San Antonio?"

"No, we are on the road to Cala Fuerte." After a little, he
added, "You've never been to the island? And yet your father
lives here?"

Selina watched the slow-moving sails of a windmill. "No.
No, I've never been."

45

"You will like Cala Fuerte. It is small, but very beautiful. A lot of yachtsmen go there."

"My father is a yachtsman." She said it without thinking, but the words caught at her, as though to say a thing, to speak it aloud, make it real, and true. *My father lives at Cala Fuerte. At a house called the Casa Barco. He is a yachtsman.*

The clouds continued to spread and part and the sun drove between them and at last they began to roll out to sea where they lay, sullenly, on the edge of the horizon. The island was bathed in warmth. Selina pushed up the sleeves of her sensible jersey dress and rolled down the window and let the scented dusty wind tear at her hair. They passed through little villages, and gold stone towns, shuttered and quiet. Doors of houses stood open, hung with curtains of chain, and on the pavement old ladies sat, upright in kitchen chairs, talking or watching their little grandchildren, their worn hands busy with embroidery and lace-making.

They came to Curamayor, a sleepy town of creamy houses and narrow streets, and Toni rubbed the back of his hand across his mouth and announced that he was feeling thirsty.

Selina, not quite sure what was expected of her, said nothing.

"Some beer would be good," Toni went on.

"I . . . I would buy you a beer, but I haven't any money."

"I will buy a beer," said Toni. The narrow street opened into a large cobbled square, with a tall church, and shady trees, and some shops. He cruised gently round until he saw a café which met with his approval. "This will do."

"I . . . I'll wait for you."

"You should have something too. Driving is hot and dry. I will give you a drink." She began to protest, but he only added, "Your father will pay me back."

She sat in the sunshine at a small iron table. Behind her, inside the bar, Toni was talking to the proprietor. A small gang

of children, fresh from school, approached. They were delicious, in blue cotton pinafores and spotless white socks. They
all seemed beautiful—the little girls pin-neat with braided
dark hair and gold rings in their ears, their limbs olive-gold
and perfectly formed, and when they smiled, their teeth
showed pointed and white.

They saw Selina watching them, and were convulsed with
giggles. Two of the little girls, more forward than the others,
stopped in front of her, their grape-dark eyes dancing with fun.
She longed to make friends, and on an impulse, opened her
bag and took out a propelling pencil, never liked, about three
inches long and with a tassel of yellow and blue. She held it
out, inviting one of them to take it. At first they were too shy,
and then the little one with plaits, tentatively, as though it
might bite, removed it from Selina's palm. The other, with a
gesture wholly disarming, laid her own hand in Selina's, as
though she were bestowing a gift. The hand was chubby and
smooth and wore a little gold ring.

Toni came back through the chain curtains with his beer
and an orange drink for Selina, and the children took fright,
and scattered like pigeons, running and taking the tasselled
pencil with them. Enchanted, she watched them go, and Toni
said, "The little ones . . ." with as much pride and affection in
his voice as if the children had been his own.

Their journey continued. The character of the island had,
by now, completely changed, and the road ran along the base
of a range of mountains, while to seaward the fields sloped
down in a shallow curve towards a distant misty horizon. They
had been on the road nearly three hours when Selina saw the
cross, high on a mountain ahead of them, silhouetted against
the sky.

"Where is that?" she asked.

"That is the Cross of San Estaban."

"Just a cross? On top of a mountain?"

"No, there is a very big monastery. A closed order."

The village of San Estaban lay at the foot of the mountain, in the shadow of the monastery. At the crossroads in the centre of the town a sign pointed, at last, to Cala Fuerte, the first that Selina had seen. Toni swung the car down to the right, and the road sloped before them, running downhill through fields of cactus and olive groves and clusters of scented eucalyptus trees. Ahead the coast seemed thickly wooded with pine, but as they drew near, Selina glimpsed the white of scattered houses, and the bright pinks and blues and scarlets of the flower-filled gardens.

"Is this Cala Fuerte?"

"Sí."

"It doesn't look like the other villages."

"No, it is a resort. For visitors. Many people have villas here, for the summer, you know? They come in the hot weather from Madrid and Barcelona."

"I see."

The pines closed about them, cool shadows and the smell of resin. They passed a farmyard, noisy with chickens, a house or two, a little wine shop, and then the road opened out into a small square, built around a single spreading pine. On one side was a shop, with vegetables piled at the door, and the window filled with rope-soled shoes, camera films, straw hats and post-cards. On the other, white-washed to blinding brightness, was a house of Moorish curves and shadows, fronted by a paved terrace, furnished with tables and chairs. Over the door swung a sign, "Cala Fuerte Hotel."

Toni stopped the taxi beneath the shade of the tree and switched off the engine. Dust settled and it was very quiet.

"We are here," he said. "This is Cala Fuerte."

They got out of the car, and the coolness of the sea-breeze was welcome. There were few people about. A woman came out of the shop to gather potatoes out of a basket and put them in a paper bag. Some children played with a dog. A couple of visitors, wearing home-knitted cardigans, and obviously En-

48

glish, sat on the terrace of the hotel and wrote postcards. They looked up and saw Selina, recognized her as a fellow-country-woman, and hastily averted their eyes.

They went into the hotel, Toni leading the way. Beyond the chain curtain was a bar, very fresh and clean and cool, white-washed, with rugs on the stone floors and a rustic wooden stairway leading to an upper floor. Beneath the stair-way another door led to the back of the hotel. A dark girl with a broom was placidly shifting dust from one side of the floor to the other.

She looked up and smiled, *"Buenos días."*

"Dónde está el proprietario?"

The girl laid down her broom. *"Momento,"* she said and disappeared, soft-footed through the door under the stairway. It swung shut behind her. Toni went to hitch himself up on to one of the tall stools at the bar. After a little the door opened again and a man came in. He was small, quite young, bearded, with eyes like a friendly frog. He wore a white shirt and dark, belted trousers and a pair of blue espadrilles.

"Buenos días," he said, looking from Toni to Selina, and back again.

She said quickly, "Do you speak English?"

"Sí, señorita."

"I am sorry to bother you, but I'm looking for someone. For Mr. George Dyer."

"Yes?"

"You know him?"

He smiled and spread his hands. "Of course. You are look-ing for George? Does he know you are looking for him?"

"No. Should he?"

"Not unless you have told him you are coming."

Selina said, "It's a surprise," trying to make it sound like fun.

He seemed intrigued. "Where have you come from?"

"From London. To-day from the airport at San Antonio."

She indicated Toni, who was listening to all this with a sullen expression as if he did not like the command of the situation being taken from his hands. "The taxi-driver brought me."

"I have not seen George since yesterday. He was on his way to San Antonio."

"But, I said, we've just come from there."

"He is probably home by now. I am not certain. I have not seen him return." He grinned. "We are never sure if his car will make the long journey."

Toni cleared his throat and leaned forward. "Where can we find him?" he said.

The bearded man shrugged. "If he is in Cala Fuerte he will be at the Casa Barco."

"How can we find the Casa Barco?" The other frowned, and Toni, sensing his mild disapproval, explained. "We must find Señor Dyer, because otherwise I do not get my taxi fare paid. The Señorita has no money. . . ."

Selina swallowed. "Yes . . . yes, I'm afraid this is true. Do you think you could direct us to the Casa Barco?"

"It is too difficult. You would never find it. But," he added, "I can find someone to take you there."

"That is kind of you. Thank you so much, Mr. . . . I'm afraid I don't know your name."

"Rudolfo. Not Mr. anything. Just Rudolfo. If you wait here for a moment, I will see what I can arrange."

He went out through the curtains, across the square and into the shop opposite. Toni slumped on his stool, his bulk sagging on either side of the inadequate seat, and his mood obviously darkening. Selina began to be nervous. She said, trying to placate him, "It's annoying to be delayed, when you've been so kind. . . ."

"We do not know that Señor Dyer will be at the Casa Barco. They have not seen him return from San Antonio yet."

"Well, if he isn't, we can always wait a little. . . ."

It was the wrong thing to say. "I cannot wait. I am a working man. Time is money to me."

"Yes, of course. I do understand."

He made a sound as if to indicate that she could not possibly understand, and half turned his back to her like any overgrown and sulky schoolboy. It was a relief when Rudolfo returned. He had arranged for the son of the woman who ran the grocery store to take them to Casa Barco. The boy had a large order for Señor Dyer, which he was about to deliver on his bicycle. If they liked they could follow the bicycle in the taxi.

"Yes, of course, that will be splendid." Selina turned to Toni, and said, with a brightness she did not feel, "And he will pay your fare, and then you will be able to go straight back to San Antonio."

Toni did not look convinced, but he heaved himself off the bar stool, and followed Selina out into the square. By the taxi, a skinny boy waited by his bicycle. The handle-bars were slung with two enormous baskets, of the type used by all Spanish peasants. Badly-wrapped parcels of all shapes and sizes protruded from these baskets. Long loaves of bread, a bundle of onions, the neck of a bottle.

Rudolfo said, "This is Tomeu, the son of Maria. He will show you the way."

Like a little pilot fish, Tomeu weaved ahead, down the white-rutted road that wound with the convolutions of the coast. The island was pierced with inlets of peacock-blue water, and above the rocks could be glimpsed delectable white villas, small gardens spilling with flowers, sunbathing terraces and diving-boards.

Selina said, "I wouldn't mind living here," but Toni's mood was rapidly worsening and he would make no reply. The road was a road no longer, merely a lane winding between the mesembryanthemum-covered walls of other people's gardens. It crested a slight rise, then sloped towards a final and much larger inlet, where a tiny harbour sheltered a few fishing-boats, and quite big yachts were moored out in deep water.

The lane ran down to the backs of houses. Tomeu, ahead of them, waited. When he saw the taxi edge over the crest of the hill, he got off his bicycle, laid it against a wall, and began to unload the baskets.

Selina said, "That must be the house."

It did not look large. The back wall was white-washed and blank, except for a tiny slit of a window and a shuttered door, shaded by a thick, black pine. Behind the house the road branched, and ran to left and to right, along the backs of other houses. Here and there a narrow alley of stairs sliced down between the buildings towards the sea. There was a pleasantly haphazard look about it all, with washing flapping on lines and some nets put out to dry, and one or two skinny cats sitting in the sun and washing themselves.

Toni's taxi bumped and slithered the last few yards, Toni complaining meanwhile that there would be nowhere to turn, his taxi was not meant for such bad roads, he would put in a claim if any of his paintwork was scratched.

Selina scarcely listened. Tomeu had opened the green shutter door and disappeared into the house, lugging his heavy baskets. The taxi lurched to a halt and Selina scrambled out.

Toni said, "I will go and turn and come back for the money."

"Yes," said Selina absently, watching the open door. "Yes, you do that."

He accelerated so swiftly that she had to step back into the gutter to avoid having her toes run over, but when he had gone, she crossed the lane, and went, under the shade of the pine, cautiously in through the open door of the Casa Barco.

She had thought it would be a little house, but instead found herself in one large high-ceilinged room. The shutters were all closed, and it was dark and cool. There was no kitchen, but a small counter enclosed a galley, like a little bar, from the main living-space, and behind this she found Tomeu, on his knees, stacking the provisions into a refrigerator.

He looked up and smiled as she leaned over the counter. She said, "Señor Dyer?"

He shook his head. "No *aquí.*"

No *aquí.* Not here. Her heart sank. He wasn't back from San Antonio, and somehow she was going to have to fob Toni off with excuses, and suggestions that he be patient, when neither of them had any idea for how long they would have to wait.

Tomeu said something. Selina stared uncomprehending. To show what he meant, he came out from the little galley and went over to the far wall and began to undo the shutters and fling them wide. A blast of light and sunshine invaded the house and everything sprang into colour. The south wall, that faced out over the harbour, was almost all window, but louvred double doors opened out on to a terrace, shaded by a split-cane awning. There was a low wall, and a few battered crocks and urns, containing geraniums, and beyond the wall, the shimmering blue of the sea.

The house itself was divided in a novel way. There were no interior walls, but the roof of the galley formed a little gallery with a wooden railing and this was reached by an open flight of steps like a ship's ladder. Beneath the ship's ladder another door led into a minuscule wash-room. A hole high in the wall provided light and ventilation, and there was a sink and a lavatory and a primitive-looking shower, and a shelf with bottles and toothpaste and stuff, and a mirror, and on the floor a round washing-basket.

The rest of the space was a lofty living-room of singular charm, white-washed, and with a stone floor, scattered with bright rugs. In one corner of the room was a wide triangular fireplace, filled with fragrant wood ashes, which looked as though they needed only the lightest puff of air to bring them back to burning life. The hearth was perhaps eighteen inches from the floor, just the right height for a comfortable seat, and this continued along the wall in a sort of shelf which was scattered with cushions and rugs, piles of books, a lamp, a piece of rope in the process of being spliced, a pile of papers and magazines and a box of empty bottles.

In front of the fireplace, with its back to the terrace and the sea, was an enormous sagging couch, with room for six and no trouble at all. It was loose-covered in fading blue linen, and draped in a red-and-white-striped blanket. On the other side of the room, at right angles to the light, stood a cheap knee-hole desk, laden with more paper, a typewriter, an open box of what looked like unopened letters, and a pair of binoculars. There was a sheet of paper in the typewriter and Selina could not resist a peep.

"George Dyer's New Novel," she read. "The lazy fox jumped over the something or other hound."

And than a row of asterisks and an exclamation mark.

She turned down the corners of her mouth. So much for Mr. Rutland's hopes!

Between the galley and the door was a well, with a wrought-iron hook for the bucket and a wide shelf on which stood a half-empty bottle of wine and a cactus plant. Selina looked down and saw the dark gleam of water, and smelt it, sweet and good, and wondered if it was fit to drink; but Grandmother had always said you must never drink water abroad unless it was boiled, and this was no time to risk getting gastro-enteritis.

She left the well and came to stand in the middle of the room, looking up at the gallery. The temptation to investigate proved irresistible, and she climbed the ladder, and found a beguiling slope-ceilinged bedroom with an immense carved double bedstead (how had they ever got it up here?) placed, in state, beneath the high pitch of the gable. There was little room for more furniture, but a pair of sea-chests had been fitted in against the low walls, and a bulging curtain did duty

54

as a wardrobe. There was an upended orange box for a bedside table, its shelves filled with books, and a lamp and a transistor radio, and a ship's chronometer.

From the terrace Tomeu called "Señorita!" and Selina went down the ladder to join him. He was sitting on the wall, in the company of an enormous white Persian cat. He turned to smile at Selina, gathering up the cat in his arms as though to give it to her.

"Señor Dyer," he said, indicating the cat, which mewed pathetically, and after a struggle, leapt lightly away, stalking into a sunny corner to settle itself in dignity, wrapping its tail around its front paws.

"It is very big," said Selina. Tomeu frowned. "Big," she said again, indicating with her arms a cat the size of a tiger. "Big."

Tomeu laughed. "*Sí Muy grande.*"

"It's Señor Dyer's cat?"

"*Sí.* Señor Dyer."

She went to join him, leaning out over the wall. There was a little triangle of rocky garden with a gnarled olive tree or two, and Selina realised that, like any house built on a steep slope, the Casa Barco went in stages and the terrace was, in fact, the roof of a boathouse, with slipways which ran down to the water. A flight of steps led from the terrace to the lower level, and directly below them two men squatted, cleaning fish. Their knives sliced precisely, the blades glinting in the sunlight. They rinsed the fish in the sea, stirring up the still, jade water. Tomeu stooped to pick up a chip of stone, and threw it down at the men, and the two faces turned up to see who it was, and saw Tomeu and smiled.

"*Hombre,* Tomeu!"

He replied with some impudent back-chat, for they laughed and then went back to their work. Beneath Selina's hands the stone wall was warm, and some of the white-wash had smudged off on to the front of her dress, like chalk from a blackboard. She turned to sit on the wall, with her back to the sea, and saw the washing-line, slung between two hooks, with a row of bone-dry wrinkled clothes. A faded blue work-shirt, a pair of bathing-trunks, some white ducks with patches on the knees, and a pair of old tennis shoes worn to a shred and tied over the line by their laces. The terrace also sported a few articles of furniture, but not the *House & Garden* type. A ratty old cane chair and a wooden paint-chipped table and the sort of booby-trap deck-chair that collapses when you sit in it. She wished that she could speak Spanish and talk to the friendly Tomeu. She wanted to ask about Señor Dyer. What sort of a man was he? Which of the yachts was his? When did Tomeu think he would be back from San Antonio? But before she could start up any sort of communication with him, the sound of Toni's returning taxi came like a knell of doom. It stopped by the door and in a moment Toni came into the house, looking ill-tempered and more villainous than ever. Selina had to tell herself that he couldn't eat her. She said, firmly, "Señor Dyer is not back."

Toni received this information in frigid silence. Then he produced a toothpick and delved about at a troublesome back molar. He wiped the toothpick on the seat of his pants, put it back into his pocket and said, "What the hell we do now?"

"I shall wait here. He can't be long. Rudolfo said that he wouldn't be long. And you can either wait here too, or you can leave me your name and address and return to San Antonio. Either way I shall see that you get paid."

Unconsciously she spoke in her grandmother's voice, and to her own surprise, it worked. Toni resigned himself to the situation. He sucked his teeth for a moment or two more and than announced his decision.

"I shall wait too. But not here. At the hotel."

There was cognac at the hotel and he could have a siesta in the taxi, beneath the shade of the tree. It was half past two already and he did not enjoy being awake at half past two. "When Señor Dyer is here, you can come and tell me."

Selina could have hugged him in relief, but she only said, "Very well, I'll certainly do that." And then added, because he looked so despondent, "I am sorry this has happened, but it will be all right."

He shrugged hugely, sighing, and went back to his car. They heard him start up and drive back over the hill towards the Cala Fuerte hotel. Selina had time to think "Poor Rudolfo," and then she went back to Tomeu.

"I stay here," she told him.

He frowned. *"Usted aquí."*

"Yes. Here." She pointed to the ground. Tomeu grinned his comprehension and went to collect his empty baskets.

"Good-bye, Tomeu, and thank you."

"Adiós, Señorita."

He was gone, and Selina was alone. She went out on to the terrace and told herself that she was waiting for her father, but it was still not quite believable. She wondered if he would know, without being told, who she was. And if he did not know, she wondered how she would tell him.

It was very hot. The sun beat down on to the sheltered terrace, and she could not remember ever having been so hot. Her nylon stockings and her leather shoes and her woollen dress became, all at once, unbearable. They were no longer sensible, but unsuitable to a degree that was lunatic.

But Grandmother couldn't stand bare legs, even with a summer dress, and gloves she considered essential. *You can tell a lady by her gloves. Such an untidy-looking gel, going about without a hat.*

But Grandmother was dead. Loved, mourned, but undoubtedly dead. The voice was stilled, the dogmatic opinions would never be uttered again, and Selina was on her own, to do what she wanted, in her father's house and a world away from Queen's Gate. She went into the house, and stripped off her stockings and her shoes, and then, feeling cool and delightfully free, went in search of food. There was butter in the refrigerator, and she put some on a slice of bread, and took a tomato and a bottle of cold soda water. This picnic she ate on the terrace, perched on the wall, and watching the boats in the harbour. Afterwards, she began to be sleepy, but she did not want to be found asleep. There was something very unguarded about being found asleep. She would have to sit somewhere hard and uncomfortable and stay awake.

In the end, she climbed the ladder to the gallery and settled herself, in a certain amount of discomfort, on the top step. After a little, the huge white cat came in out of the sun, and climbed up to settle himself, with an inordinate amount of purring and treading paws, on Selina's knee.

The hands of her watch went slowly round.

5

Frances Dongen said, "I can't think why you have to go."

"I've told you; I have to feed Pearl."

"Pearl can feed herself. There are enough dead fish around that house of yours to feed an army of cats. Stay another night, darling."

"It isn't just Pearl; it's *Eclipse* as well. . . ."

"But she's ridden out one storm. . . ."

"I don't know that she has ridden it out, and the bad weather's coming back. . . ."

"Oh, well," said Frances, and reached for another cigarette. "If that's how you feel, you'd better go."

Her mother had told her, years ago, when she was a girl in Cincinnati, Ohio, that the best way to keep a man was to give him the impression, at least, of being free. Not that she had yet reached the stage of keeping George Dyer, because she hadn't even got him yet, but she was an old hand at this fascinating game of stalk and counter-stalk, and she was prepared to take her time.

She was sitting, on the small terrace of her house, high in the old town of San Antonio. Above, only a few hundred yards or so separated her from the cathedral, and below, a maze of winding cobbled streets, tall, narrow houses, and endless strings of washing, spilled to the wall of the old fortifications. Beyond the wall lay the new town, wide streets and tree-lined squares leading to the harbour, filled with island schooners and white, tall-masted yachts, and the steamer, which had just arrived on its weekly trip from Barcelona.

For two years she had lived in this delectable spot, ever since she had arrived in the cruising yacht of some wealthy American friends. After six weeks of their company, Frances was bored stiff, and when they all came ashore for a party, she never left again. After a three-day binge, she had woken to a monumental hangover and a strange bed, and the realisation that the cruising yacht and all its occupants had left without her.

This troubled Frances not in the least. She already seemed to have made a lot of new friends, she was rich, twice-married, without roots. San Antonio suited her down to the ground. It was filled with painters, expatriates, writers and beatniks, and Frances, who had once lived for several months with an unsuccessful artist in Greenwich Village, felt entirely at home. Before long she had found this house, and when the initial occupations of settling-in were over, cast about for some way of filling in her time. She decided upon an art gallery. In a place where you had both resident painters and visiting tourists, an art gallery was surely a blue-chip investment. She bought up a disused fish-market on the harbour, converted it, and managed the business with an acumen she had inherited not only from her father, but from her two ex-husbands as well.

She was not nearly forty, but everything about her belied the passing of years. Tall, very thin, tanned like a boy, with her blonde head a tangle of artless curls, she wore, and got away with, the sort of clothes normally reserved for teenagers. Tight pants, and men's shirts, and bikinis that were no more than a couple of knotted handkerchiefs. She chain-smoked, and she knew she was drinking too much, but most of the time, and this morning in particular, life was just as good as she'd always meant it to be.

The party last night, thrown in honour of Olaf Svensen's first exhibition, had been particularly successful. Olaf was the dirtiest young man ever seen, even by San Antonio standards, with a scrofulous beard and toe-nails that scarcely bore looking at, but his pop-art sculpture was guaranteed to open eyes, and Frances took a certain mild pleasure in shocking the public. George Dyer had certainly been asked to the party—since the publication of his book he had become something of a celebrity—but that was no guarantee that he would come, and Frances's spirits had soared in pleasure when she saw him come through the door and start to thread his way towards her through the crowded smoke-filled room. He told her that he was in San Antonio to pick up a spare part for his boat, and after hearing his comments on Olaf's work, she knew that he had only come to the party for the free drink, but what did it matter provided he was there, and what was more, had stayed, right to the end of the party, and then afterwards, with Frances. She had known him, now, for about a year. Last spring, she had driven over to Cala Fuerte to look at the work of a young French painter who lived there. She had wound up, inevitably, in Rudolfo's bar, standing the painter a string of martinis, but when George Dyer walked in, she had abandoned the Frenchman, who went to sleep with his head on the table, and started to talk to George instead, and they ended up having lunch together, and were still drinking coffee at six o'clock in the evening, when it was time to switch back to brandy again.

He usually came to San Antonio about once a week, to pick up his mail from the Yacht Club, and go to the bank, and stock up on supplies for his boat, and on these occasions he nearly always looked Frances up, and they would have dinner, or attach themselves to some party already in full swing in one of the waterside bars. She was enormously attracted by him— more so, she knew, than he was to her, but this only served to make him all the more desirable. It made her jealous, too, of his other interests, of anything that kept him away from her. His writing, his yacht, but most of all the self-contained existence he led at Cala Fuerte. She would have liked him to need her, but he seemed to need nothing. He was unimpressed by her money, but delighted in her coarse and very masculine sense of humor. Watching him now, she thought, with satisfaction, that he was the first real man she had met in years.

He was getting ready to go, packing the things he had bought into a basket. Just watching his brown hands perform this homely task made Frances ache with physical desire. She said, against her better judgment, but hoping to make him stay a little longer, "You've had nothing to eat."

"I'll get something at home."

At home. She wished this were his home. She said, "A drink?"

He laughed, and looked up at her, distinctly bloodshot and amused as hell. "Look, ducky, I have a three-hour drive."

"A drink wouldn't kill you." She wanted one herself.

"No, but a ruddy great truck might, after I'd gone to sleep."

The basket was packed. He stood up and said, "I must go."

Frances stood too, stooped to stub out her cigarette and went to help him with his things. He lifted the heavy crate with the spare propeller, and Frances carried the basket, and led the way down the stone stairs to her enclosed courtyard, where the lemon tree grew by the well. She opened the heavy double doors that led to the narrow street, and stepped out in the sunshine. Here, on the crazy slope of the hill, George's ridiculous car was parked, an ancient Morris Cowley, with yellow wheels and a hood like a perambulator. They loaded it up, and George turned to say good-bye.

"It's been fun," he said.

"That's because we didn't plan it, darling. What's the word? Spontaneous." She kissed his mouth. She was so tall that she did not have to reach up to do it, merely leaned forward and caught him unawares. She wore a bright, thick lipstick that came off on his mouth and tasted sweet, and when she drew away, he wiped the stain away on the back of his hand.

He got into the car.

"Good-bye, darling."

" 'Bye, Frances."

" 'Bye."

She removed the stone which, last night, feeble with laughter, they had jammed beneath the front wheel, and George took off the brake and the car free-wheeled away, gathering terrifying speed as it went, and taking the corners of the narrow, steep street like a helter-skelter at the fair, scattering cats and chickens and causing the Guardia Civil, posted at the gate of the old wall, to suck their teeth in violent disapproval.

He bowled back to Cala Fuerte, down the dusty roads, through the neatly-tended fields, past the windmills, and the patient horses turning the water-wheels. He came to the winding road beneath the mountains, and the cross of San Estaban towered above him. He squinted out to sea for signs of the returning storm, and he thought about Frances. He thought of going to live in San Antonio with Frances, if only for the satisfaction of writing to Rutland, the publisher, and telling him to go to hell, he wasn't going to write any more books, he was going to become a beachcomber, a lotus-eater, he was going to be kept by a rich American.

At San Estaban, the siesta was over, the shutters had been thrown wide and a few peaceful customers sat outside the cafés. As George passed, tooting the horn of the car, they called *"Hombre!"* and waved, because they all knew him, if not by name, then by sight, because he was the mad Englishman in the little car with yellow wheels, who drove around the island wearing a yacthing cap and sometimes wrote books.

As he came free-wheeling down the last stretch of road that led to Cala Fuerte, he had a small debate with himself as to whether or not he would call in at Rudolfo's for a drink. In the end, rather to his own surprise, he decided against it. He would undoubtedly meet friends, would stay longer than he intended, would drink more than was good for him. He did not trust the weather, and Pearl would be hungry; so instead, he compromised with a friendly toot on his horn as he came through the square, and a genial wave to anybody who might be sitting on the terrace of the Cala Fuerte. There was no sign of Rudolfo, but one or two startled drinkers waved back, and there was the good feeling of coming home, and George began to whistle.

He was whistling when he came into the house. Selina, still sitting on the ladder, heard the car come over the hill, and down the slope, and stop, with a great screeching of ancient brakes, outside the Casa Barco. She sat motionless, the white cat, a great, heavy weight, asleep in her lap. The car engine was switched off, and it was then that she heard the whistling. A door opened and was slammed shut. The whistling continued, grew louder. The door of the Casa Barco was pushed open, and a man came in.

He carried a basket in one hand, a cardboard box under the other arm, and a roll of newspapers in his teeth. He shut the door with the seat of his pants, put the basket down on the floor, took the papers out of his mouth and dropped them into the basket, and then carried the box to the table by the type-writer and set it carefully down. She couldn't see his face, because it was obscured by the peak of his battered, faintly sea-going cap, but he opened the top of the box, and checked, amongst paper shavings, on the contents. Seemingly content, he then picked up the binoculars and disappeared out on to the terrace. Selina sat still, where she was, but the cat began to wake up. She stroked it, partly out of nervousness, and partly because she didn't want it to move. After a little, he came back into the house again, laid down the binoculars and took off his cap and threw it down on the table. He had dark hair, very thick and just beginning to be run through with grey. His shirt was the faded blue one of any farmer, his pants washed-out khaki denim, his shoes a pair of dusty espadrilles. Still whistling, he went back to collect the basket and take it into the galley, disappearing once more from Selina's view. She heard him open and shut the refrigerator door, there was the sound of a bottle being opened, the chink of glass, the pouring of a drink. When he appeared once more he was carrying a tumbler of what looked like soda water. He went back out on to the terrace and called "Pearl!" The cat began to stretch its legs. "Pearl! Pearley!" He made seductive kissing noises. The cat mewed. He came back into the house. "Pearl."

Selina ran a tongue over her lips, took a deep breath, and said, "Are you looking for the cat?"

George Dyer stopped dead in his tracks and looked up and saw the girl, sitting at the top of the steps. She had long bare legs and bare feet, and Pearl, like a huge white fur cush-ion, lay on her knee.

He frowned slightly, trying to remember. He said, "Were you there just now, when I came through?"

"Yes."

"I never saw you."

"No, I know you didn't." He told himself that her voice was very well modulated, very nicely brought up. She went on, "Is Pearl the name of your cat?"

"Yes, I came back to feed her."

"She's been sitting on my knee all afternoon."

"All after— . . . How long have you been here?"

"Since half past two."

"Half past two?" He glanced at his watch. "But it's past five o'clock."

"Yes, I know."

Pearl now took a hand in the conversation by sitting up, stretching, uttering another plaintive mew, and springing lightly out of the girl's lap and down the steps. Purring like a kettle, she wrapped herself around George's legs, but for once was ignored.

"Are you here for any particular reason?"

"Oh, yes, I came to see you."

"Well, wouldn't it be a good idea to come down off that ladder?"

She did so. She stood up, obviously very stiff, and descended a step at a time, trying to push her hair back from her face. After Frances Dongen, and all the other suntanned young ladies at San Antonio, she looked very pale, with straight fawn-coloured hair that hung to her shoulders and a fringe to her eyebrows. Her eyes were blue, but shadowed with tiredness. He thought that she was too young even to be pretty.

He said, "I don't even know you . . . do I?"

"No. No, you don't. I hope you don't mind my just walking into your house."

"Not at all."

"The door wasn't bolted."

"It doesn't have any bolts."

Selina smiled, thinking perhaps this was a joke, but it apparently wasn't, so she stopped smiling, and tried to think what to say next. Subconsciously, she had been waiting for him to recognise her, to say "Who do you remind me of?" or "But, of course, I've met you before, some time, somewhere." But none of these remarks was forthcoming, and she found his appearance disconcerting, with no suggestion of the bright-eyed, clean-cut young officer who had been her father. She had expected him to be very brown, but she had not realised that his face would be so lined, or his dark eyes so bloodshot. The fact that he needed a shave not only hid the clean line of his jaw and the cleft of his chin, but added to his villainous appearance. Furthermore he did not seem in the least pleased to see her.

She swallowed, "I . . . expect you're wondering why I'm here."

"Well, yes, I am, but I've no doubt that in time you'll tell me."

"I flew here, from London . . . this morning, last night. No, this morning."

He was visited with a horrible suspicion. "Did Rutland send you?"

"Who? Oh, Mr. Rutland the publisher. No, he didn't, but he did say that he wished you'd answer his letters."

"The devil he did." Another thought occurred to him. "But you do know him?"

"Oh, yes, I went to see him and ask him how I could find you."

"But who are you?"

"My name's Selina Bruce."

"I'm George Dyer, but I imagine you know that."

"Yes, I know. . . ."

There was another silence. George, despite himself began to be intrigued. "You couldn't be a fan? You couldn't be the Organising Secretary of the George Dyer Fan Club." Selina shook her head. "Then you're staying at the Cala Fuerte Hotel and you've read my book?" She shook her head again. "This is

67

like Twenty Questions, isn't it? Are you famous? Are you an actress? Do you sing?"

"No, but I had to see you, because . . ." Her courage left her. "Because," she finished, "I have to ask you to lend me six hundred pesetas."

George Dyer felt his own jaw sag with astonishment, and hastily laid down the glass of soda water before he should drop it.

"What did you say?"

"Do you have," said Selina, sounding very clear and highly pitched, as though she were talking to someone suffering from deafness, "six hundred pesetas you could lend me?"

"Six hundred!" He laughed. He laughed without mirth. "You must be joking."

"I only wish I were."

"Six hundred pesetas! I don't have twenty pesetas!"

"But I must have six hundred, to pay the taxi-driver."

George looked around him. "Where does the taxi-driver come into it?"

"I had to get a taxi from the Aeropuerto to Cala Fuerte. I told the taxi-driver that you would pay him because I hadn't got any money. My wallet was stolen at the Aeropuerto, while I was waiting to see if they could find my luggage. . . . Look. . . ." She went to pick up her handbag, and show him the two clear-cut edges of the handles. "The Guardia Civil said it must have been a very experienced thief, because I didn't feel a thing, and it was only my wallet that was taken."

"Only your wallet. And what did your wallet contain?"

"My traveller's cheques, and some British money, and some pesetas. And," she added, with the air of one determined to make a clean breast of it, "my return ticket."

"I see," said George.

"And the taxi-driver is waiting now, at the Cala Fuerte Hotel. For you. To pay him."

"You mean, you took a taxi from the Aeropuerto to Cala Fuerte to find me in order to pay the taxi fare. It's crazy. . . ."

"But I've explained. . . . You see, my luggage never came. . . ."

"You mean, you lost your luggage as *well!*"

"I didn't lose my luggage—*they* did. The air line."

"That's jet travel for you. Breakfast in London, lunch in Spain, luggage in Bombay."

"It got to Barcelona, but they think it must have been sent to Madrid."

"So," said George with the air of an efficient quizmaster doing a re-cap, "your luggage is in Madrid, and your wallet has been stolen and you want six hundred pesetas to pay your taxi fare."

"Yes," said Selina, delighted that he at last grasped the situation.

"And what did you say your name was?"

"Selina Bruce."

"Well, Miss Bruce, delighted though I am to have made your acquaintance, and naturally distressed to learn of your run of bad luck, I still don't see what it has to do with me."

"I think it has a lot to do with you," said Selina.

"Oh, you do?"

"Yes. You see. . . . I think I'm your daughter."

"You think . . ."

His first reaction was that she was insane. She had to be. She was one of those lunatic women who go round insisting they're the Empress Eugénie, only this one had a fixation about him.

"Yes. I think you're my father."

She wasn't insane. She was entirely innocent and she really believed what she was saying. He told himself that he must be rational. "What ever gave you that idea?"

"I have a little photograph of my father. I thought he was dead. But he has the same face as you."

"That's bad luck on him."

"Oh, no, it isn't bad at all. . . ."

"Have you got the photograph?"

"Yes, it's right here. . . ." She stooped to pick up her bag again, and he tried to reckon how old she was; he tried to remember, to decide, in a frenzied life-and-death sort of way, whether there could be the slightest chance that this dreadful accusation might be true. "It's here . . . I've always carried it around with me, ever since I found it, about five years ago. And then when I saw the photograph on the back of your book . . ." She held it out to him. He took it, not taking his eyes off her face. He said, "How old are you?"

"Twenty."

Relief made him feel quite weak. To hide the expression in his face he looked quickly down at the photograph that Selina had handed him. He did not say anything. And then, as Rodney had done when Selina first showed it to him, George Dyer carried it over to the light. After a little, he said, "What was his name?"

Selina swallowed. "Gerry Dawson. But the same initials as you."

"Could you tell me something about him?"

"Not very much. You see, I was always told that he was killed before I was born. My mother was called Harriet Bruce, and she died just *after* I was born, so my grandmother brought me up and that's why I'm called Selina Bruce."

"Your grandmother. Your mother's mother."

"Yes."

"And you found this photograph . . . ?"

"Five years ago. In a book of my mother's. And then I . . . was given *Fiesta at Cala Fuerte*, and I saw your photograph on the back, and it seemed to be the same. The same face, I mean. The same. The same person."

George Dyer did not reply. He came back from the open door, and gave her back the photograph. Then he lit a cigarette, and when he had shaken out the match, and placed it, dead centre, in the middle of the ash-tray, he said, "You said you were told he was killed. What do you mean by that?"

"Because I *was* told that. But I've always known that my grandmother didn't like him. She never wanted him to marry my mother. And when I saw the photograph, I thought perhaps there'd been some mistake. That he hadn't been killed at all. That he'd been wounded or something, lost his memory. That did happen, you know."

"But not to your father. Your father is dead."

"But you . . ."

He said, very gently, "I'm not your father."

"But . . ."

"You're twenty. I'm thirty-seven. I probably look a great deal more, but, in fact, I'm only thirty-seven. I wasn't even in the war—not that one, anyway."

"But the photographs . . ."

"I have an idea that Gerry Dawson was a second cousin of mine. The fact that we look alike is one of those freaks of heredity. In fact, I think we probably weren't all that alike. The photograph of your father, and the picture on the back of my book, were taken years apart. And even in my hey-day, I was never as good-looking as that."

Selina stared at him. She had never seen a man so brown, and someone needed to sew a button on his shirt because it was open right down, so that you could see the dark hair on his chest, and the sleeves of the shirt were rolled up to just below his elbows, as though he couldn't be bothered to make a proper job of them. She felt curious, as though she would have no control over anything her body might choose to do. Her legs might buckle, her eyes fill with tears, she might even start hitting him, as he stood there, telling her that he wasn't her father. That it was all true, and Gerry Dawson was dead.

He was still talking, sounding as if he was trying to be kind. ". . . sorry you've come all this way. Don't feel too

71

badly about it . . . it's a mistake that could easily be made
. . . after all . . ."

There was a lump in her throat that ached, and his face,
so close to her own, began to blur and swim as though it was
sinking into the bottom of a pond. She had been far too warm,
but now, suddenly, she was freezing cold, her arms and her
back and the very roots of her hair were crawling with goose
pimples. He said, and he seemed to be speaking from a great
distance, "Are you all right?" and she realised to her shame
that she was not after all going to faint, nor attack him in rage,
but simply dissolve, ignominiously, into tears.

6

She said, "I suppose you haven't got such a thing as a handkerchief?"

He hadn't, but he went and fetched a large box of Kleenex and thrust it into her hands. She pulled one out and blew her nose, and said, "I don't think I'm going to need them all."

"I wouldn't be too sure."

"I am sorry. I didn't mean to do that. Cry, I mean."

"I'm sure you didn't."

She took another paper tissue and blew her nose again. "I'd been waiting so long. And it was suddenly so cold."

"It is colder. The sun's gone. There's been another storm warning. Here, come and sit down."

He put a hand under her elbow and propelled her to the gargantuan couch, and because she was still shivering, pulled the red-and-white blanket down over her knees and said that

73

he would get her some brandy. Selina said she didn't like brandy, but he went just the same, and she watched him, behind the counter of his little galley, finding a bottle and a glass and pouring her a drink.

When he brought it back, she said, "I really need something to eat."

"Drink this first, anyway."

The glass was small and thick, and the brandy neat. Selina shuddered. When it was finished, he took the empty glass, and, on his way back to the galley, kicked up the ashes in the fireplace and tossed on another piece of driftwood. The ashes rose and fell again, coating the fresh piece of wood with grey dust. Presently, as Selina watched, there was a glow of red and a tiny flame.

She said, "You don't even need to use bellows . . . it's burning up already."

"They know how to build a fireplace here. What do you want to eat?"

"I don't mind."

"Soup. Bread and butter. Cold meat. Fruit."

"Have you got some soup?"

"A can. . . ."

"Isn't that a nuisance?"

"Less of a nuisance than having you in tears."

Selina was hurt, and said, "I didn't mean to."

When the soup was heating, he came back to sit on the edge of the hearth and talk to her. "Whereabouts do you live?" he asked, reaching for a cigarette, and lighting it with a spill from the fire.

"In London."

"With your grandmother?"

"My grandmother's dead."

"You don't live alone?"

"No. There's Agnes."

"Who's Agnes?"

"My Nanny," said Selina, and immediately could have bitten out her tongue. "I mean . . . she used to be my Nanny."

"Isn't there anyone else?"

"Yes," said Selina. "There's Rodney."

"Who's Rodney?"

Selina's eyes widened. "He's my . . . lawyer."

"Does anybody know you're out here?"

"Agnes knows I was coming."

"And the lawyer . . . ?"

"He was away. On business."

"Then there's nobody to worry about you? To wonder where you are."

"No."

"Well, that's something."

The soup in the pan began to bubble. George Dyer went back to the galley to find a bowl and a spoon, and Selina said, "I like your house."

"Do you?"

"Yes. It's got a nice feeling, as though it just happened. As though it wasn't ever planned."

She thought of the flat in London where she and Rodney were going to live when they were married. Of the time and the thought that was being put into the carpets and the curtains and the right lighting and cushions, and the wastepaper baskets, and the kitchen and the pots and the pans. She said, "I think that's the way a house should be. It should evolve. Like the people who live in it." George Dyer was pouring himself out a whisky and soda and did not reply. She went on, "You have to have some things, of course, a roof over your head, and a fire, and . . . I suppose, somewhere to sleep." He came back from the galley, carrying the bowl of soup, with a spoon sticking out of it, in one hand, and his drink in the other. Selina took the soup bowl and said, "How did you get the bed up into the gallery?"

"In pieces. We put it together up there."

"It's very large."

"In Spain it's called a *Matrimoniale*. A marriage bed."

She was slightly embarrassed. "I couldn't think how you'd got it up there. I . . . I shouldn't have looked, I'm sorry, but I wanted to see everything before you came."

He said, "What are you going to do now?"

Selina looked down at her soup, stirring it. It was vegetable soup with alphabet noodles floating around it. She said, "I suppose I'd better go home."

"With no ticket and no money?"

"If I could borrow some, I could go back to San Antonio with Toni in his taxi. And I could catch the next flight back to London."

George said, "I really was telling you the truth when I said I hadn't got that six hundred pesetas. One of the reasons I went to San Antonio yesterday was to pick up some cash, but there's been some delay at the clearing bank in Barcelona, and at the moment I'm cleaned out."

"But what am I going to do about the taxi-driver? I have to pay him."

"Perhaps Rudolfo at the Cala Fuerte will help us."

"It seems a lot to ask."

"He's used to it."

"It isn't just the six hundred pesetas for the taxi. I'll have to buy another air ticket."

"Yes, I know."

The soup was still too hot to drink. Selina stirred it again, and said, "You must think I'm the most awful fool." He did not deny this, and she went on, "Of course I should have written or something, but I couldn't bear the thought of waiting for a reply." He still made no comment, and she felt she must try to justify herself. "You'd think that you'd get used to not having a father, particularly if you'd never known him. But I never did get used to it. I used to think about it all the time. Rodney said I had an obsession about it."

"It's not a bad thing to have an obsession about."

"I showed Agnes the photograph on the back of your book, and she was struck all of a heap, because you look so like my father. That's what really made me come, because Agnes knew him very well. And I wouldn't seem quite so stupid if I hadn't had my wallet stolen. Up to then I'd done quite well. I caught all the right connections, and it wasn't my fault my luggage got sent to Madrid."

"Did you never travel on your own before?" He sounded incredulous.

"Oh, yes, heaps of times. But only on trains going to school and things." Something in his expression compelled her to be entirely honest. "And then there was somebody to meet me. . . ." She shrugged. "You know."

"No, I don't, but I believe you."

She began to eat the soup. She said, "If my father really was your second cousin, then we must be related."

"Second cousin once removed."

"It sounds terribly remote, doesn't it? And rather royal. Did you ever know my father?"

"No, I never knew him." He frowned. "What did you say your name was?"

"Selina."

"Selina. Well, if I ever needed proof that you're not my daughter, there it is."

"How do you mean?"

"I'd never saddle any girl with a name like that."

"What would you call her?"

"A man seldom imagines daughters. He only thinks of a son. George Dyer Junior, perhaps." He raised his glass to this mythical son, finished his drink and set down the glass. "Now, come on, eat up that soup and we'll go and find the taxi-driver."

While he piled the soup bowl and the glasses into the sink and fed the hungry Pearl, Selina washed her hands and face in the sink in his bathroom and combed her hair and put on her stockings and shoes again. When she emerged, he was out on the terrace once more, his cap on the back of his head, watching the harbour through his binoculars. Selina came to stand beside him.

"Which is your boat?"

"That one."

"What's her name?"

"*Eclipse.*"

"She looks big to sail single-handed."

"She is. I usually have a crew." He added, "I get a bit edgy when this heavy weather blows up. A hell of a sea comes in round that headland, and I've known her pull anchor."

"Surely she's safe there."

"The rocks come too far out into deep water for comfort."

She glanced at the sky. It was overcast and leaden. "Is there going to be another storm?"

"Yes, the wind's changed. It was a rotten forecast." He lowered the binoculars and looked down at her. "Did you catch the storm last night?"

"It chased us over the Pyrenees. We could scarcely land at Barcelona."

He said, "I don't mind a storm at sea, but a storm in the air scares me paralytic. Are you ready?"

"Yes."

"We'll take the car."

They went back into the house and he put down his binoculars on the desk, and Selina collected her bag and said a silent good-bye to the Casa Barco. She had thought so much about coming to it, and now, after only a few hours, she was leaving it again. For good. She picked up her coat. He said, "What the hell's that for?"

"It's my coat. It's cold in London."

"You know, I'd forgotten. Here, I'll carry it for you." He

slung it over his shoulder and added, "One thing about losing all your luggage, you do at least travel light."

They went out of the house, and Selina didn't know whether his car was meant as a joke or not. It looked as if it had been decorated for a Students' Rag Week, and she longed to ask if he had painted the wheels yellow himself, but somehow hadn't the nerve. They clambered in, and George piled Selina's coat on her knee, then started the engine, jammed in the gear, and turned the car in a series of hair-raising forward and backward jerks. Disaster loomed. At one moment they seemed about to ram a solid wall. The next, their back wheels teetered at the edge of a steep alley of steps. Selina shut her eyes. When at last they shot forward and up the hill there was an overpowering smell of exhaust, and sinister clanking sounds came from somewhere beneath her feet. The seats sagged and had holes in them, and the floor, which had lost its carpeting years ago, resembled nothing so much as the bottom of a dustbin. For George's sake, Selina hoped that his yacht was more seaworthy.

But, for all that, there was something very friendly about driving through Cala Fuerte in George Dyer's car. All the children screamed with laughter and waved, and shouted joyous salutations. All the women sitting in their gardens, or gossiping at their doors, turned to smile and send a greeting after them. All the men, sitting outside the cafés, walking home from work, stopped to let them go bowling by, with shouted pleasantries in Spanish which Selina didn't understand, but which George Dyer evidently did.

"What are they saying?"

"They want to know where I found my new Señorita."

"Is that all?"

"Isn't that enough?"

They came with a flourish up to the Cala Fuerte Hotel, and stopped so suddenly that a cloud of white dust rose from their wheels and coated the tables, and the drinks of the clients who sat on Rudolfo's terrace enjoying the first aperitifs of the evening. An Englishman was heard to say, "Bloody cheek," but George Dyer ignored him, climbed out of the car without bothering to open the door, and went up the steps of the terrace and through the chain curtain with Selina behind him.

"Rudolfo!"

Rudolfo was behind the bar. He said, in Spanish, "There is no need to shout."

"Rudolfo, where is the taxi-driver?"

Rudolfo was not smiling. He poured a tray of drinks and said, "The taxi-driver has gone."

"Gone? Didn't he want his money?"

"Yes, he wanted his money. Six hundred pesetas."

"Who paid him?"

"I did," said Rudolfo. "And I want to talk to you. Wait till I serve my customers."

He came out from behind the bar, walked past them without a word, and disappeared through the chain curtain and on to the terrace. Selina stared at George. "Is he angry?"

"At a guess I'd say he was annoyed about something."

"Where is Toni?"

"He's gone. Rudolfo paid him off."

It took a second or so for the enormity of this to sink in. "But if he's gone . . . how am I going to get back to San Antonio?"

"God knows."

"You'll have to take me."

"I am not driving back to San Antonio this evening, and even if I did, we still can't buy you a plane ticket."

Selina bit her lip. She said, "Rudolfo seemed so nice before."

"Like all of us he has two sides to his character."

Rudolfo returned, the chain curtain clashed behind him, and he put down his empty tray and turned on George.

He did it in Spanish which was perhaps just as well, for

the language he employed was not for the ears of a delicately-nurtured young English Señorita. George, with spirit, defended himself. As their voices rose, Selina, unable to ignore the obvious fact that a good deal of the references were to herself, would say, "Oh, please tell me what it's all about," or "Couldn't you say some of this in English so that I could understand?" but neither of them took the slightest notice of her.

The argument was interrupted at last by the arrival of a fat German who wanted a glass of beer, and while Rudolfo went behind the bar to serve him, Selina took the opportunity to tug at George's sleeve and say, "What's *happened?* Tell me what's happened!"

"Rudolfo is annoyed because you said you would wait at the Casa Barco, and he thought that the taxi-driver would wait there with you. He doesn't like stray taxi-drivers sitting round his bar, getting sloshed, and he seems to have taken a particular dislike to this one."

"Oh."

"Yes, oh."

"Is that all?"

"No, of course it's not all. In the end, to get rid of the man, Rudolfo paid him. And now he says I owe him six hundred pesetas, and he's got cold feet because he doesn't think I'll be able to pay him back."

"But, I'll pay him. . . . I promise. . . ."

"That isn't really the point. He wants it now."

The fat German, sensing a bad atmosphere, carried his beer outside and he was no sooner away than Rudolfo and George turned on each other once more, but Selina moved swiftly forward.

"Oh please, Mr. . . . Rudolfo, I mean. It's all my fault, and I'll see you get paid back, but you see, all my money was stolen. . . ."

Rudolfo had heard this before. "You said you would wait at the Casa Barco. With the taxi-driver."

"I didn't know he would be here for so long."

"And you," Rudolfo turned to George again. "Where were you, anyway? Going off to San Antonio, and not coming back, and nobody knows where you are . . ."

"What the hell's it got to do with you? Where I go and what I do is my own bloody business."

"It has to do with me when I have to pay your bills."

"Nobody asked you to pay it. And it wasn't my bill, anyway. And you've loused everything up, because now the Señorita can't get back to San Antonio."

"Then take her yourself!"

"I'll be damned if I will!" yelled George. And with that, he stormed out of the bar, was down the terrace steps in a single stride, and into his car. Selina shot after him. "What about me?"

He turned to look at her. "Well, are you coming or are you going to stay here?"

"I don't want to stay here."

"Come on, then."

There was no alternative. Half the village, and all Rudolfo's customers, seemed to be enjoying the scene. George leaned over to open her door, and Selina got in beside him.

At this moment, as if on a signal from some celestial stage manager, the storm broke.

There was a flash of lightning that split the sky, a roll of thunder and a sudden upsurge of wind that sent the pines shaking. The tablecloths on the Cala Fuerte terrace rose and flapped like badly-set sails, and a hat blew from the rack outside Maria's shop, and went bowling, a big pink and yellow wheel, down the main street. Dust rose in spirals, and behind the wind came the rain, a sudden sheet of it, the drops so big and heavy that in seconds the gutters were flooded.

Everybody rushed indoors. Rudolfo's customers, the gossiping women, the scampering children, the two men who had been working on the road. There was a general air of impending disaster as though an air-raid siren had gone, and in no time the place was deserted. Except for Selina and George, and George's little car.

She started to get out, but he had the engine running and he yanked her back again. She said, "Can't we shelter too?"

"What for? You're not afraid of a little rain?"

"A *little* rain?" His profile was stony and he didn't deign to answer. "Doesn't the hood go up?"

He pushed the car into gear and they started with the suddenness of an exploding rocket.

"It hasn't done for ten years," he shouted over the din of the car and the rain and the wind. Already they seemed to be up to the hubcaps in water, and Selina's feet were awash. She wondered if she should start baling.

"Well, what's the good of a hood if it doesn't go up?"

"Oh, stop bellyaching."

"I am not bellyaching, but . . ."

He accelerated, and her words died in a grasp of fright. They roared down the road, cutting corners with screeching tyres and sending up waves of yellow mud. The sea was the colour of lead, and the gardens of the delectable little villas already devastated by the wind. The air seemed to be filled with flying flotsam—leaves and scraps of straw and pine-needles—and when at last they came over the hill and down the lane towards Casa Barco, the water, penned between high walls, had reached the proportions of a deep stream, and their progress in George's car was like shooting rapids.

The bulk of this water, by force of gravity, was diverted down the flight of steps which led to the harbour, but a good deal had invaded the old net-store where he kept his car, and which already appeared to be in a state of flood.

Despite this, he drove straight into it, stopping a perilous inch from the far wall. He switched off the engine and jumped out, saying, "Come on, get out, and help me to get the doors shut."

Selina was too frightened to rebel. She stepped out into four inches of cold, dirty water and went to help him drag shut the sagging doors. They got them closed at last, leaning against them until, by sheer brute force, George was able to jam the primitive bolt into position. This done, he took her by the wrist and ran her into the Casa Barco, as another flash of lightning split the black sky to be followed by a roll of thunder so close that she thought the roof was going to fall in.

Even in the house, they did not appear to be safe. He went straight out on to the terrace, and began to struggle with the shutters. The wind was so strong that he had to prise them away from the walls of the house. The pots of flowers had already gone, some over the edge of the wall, others on to the terrace, where they lay, a mêlée of broken earthenware and spilt mud. When at last he got the shutters closed, and the inner doors, the house seemed dark and unfamiliar. He tried the light switch, but the electricity had gone off. The rain, coming down the chimney, had put out the fire, and the well was gurgling as though it might at any moment overflow.

Selina said, "Are we going to be all right?"

"Why shouldn't we be all right?"

"I'm frightened of thunder."

"It can't hurt you."

"Lightning can."

"Well, then, be frightened of lightning."

"I am. I'm frightened of that, too."

She felt that he should apologise, but he merely felt in his pocket and pulled out a soggy packet of cigarettes. He chucked this into the spitting fireplace, and went prowling, searching for more, eventually running a packet to earth in the galley. He took one and lit it, and then, while he was there, poured himself a stiff whisky. He brought the glass to the well, let down the bucket and brought it up brimfull, and, with a dexterity born of long practice, tipped the water from the bucket into the glass without spilling a drop.

He said, "Do you want a drink?"

"No, thank you."

He took a mouthful of whisky and stood watching her, and she couldn't guess if he was laughing or not. They were both of them as wet as if they had fallen into a bath. Selina had shucked off her ruined shoes and now stood in an ever-widening puddle of water with her dress-hem dripping and her hair plastered to her face and neck. Being wet did not appear to bother George Dyer as much as it bothered her. She said, "I suppose you're used to this sort of thing," and tried to wring out the hem of her dress. "There wasn't even any need for it. We could easily have sheltered till the storm was over. Rudolfo would have let us. . . ."

He set down the glass with a small clash, and went across the room, and, two at a time, up the ladder to the gallery.

"Here," he said, and threw down a pair of pyjamas. "And here." They were followed by a towelling robe. There was the sound of a drawer being opened and shut. "And here." A towel. He stood, his hands on the rail, looking down at her. "Use the bathroom. Take everything off and give yourself a rub and get changed."

Selina went to pick up the clothes. As she opened the bathroom door, a wet shirt came over the gallery rail to be followed by a soaking pair of denims. Swiftly she shot into the bathroom and locked the door.

When she emerged, dried and dressed in the over-large clothes, and with her hair wrapped in a turban of dry towel, she found a certain metamorphosis had taken place.

The fire was blazing brightly once more, and there were three or four lighted candles standing about in old wine bottles. The transistor radio was playing flamenco music, and George Dyer had not only changed and cleaned himself up, but shaved as well. He wore a white polo-necked sweater, and a pair of blue serge pants, and red leather slippers. He was sitting on the hearth with his back to the fire, reading one of his English newspapers and looking as relaxed as any gentleman in his country home. He glanced up as she came in.

"Well, there you are."

"What shall I do with all my wet things?"

"Chuck them on the bathroom floor. Juanita can cope in the morning."

"Who's Juanita?"

"My maid. Maria's sister. Do you know who Maria is? She runs the grocery store in the village."

"The mother of Tomeu."

"So you have already met Tomeu."

"Tomeu brought us here today; he led the way on his bicycle."

"Tomeu brought a chicken in that big basket of groceries. It's in the oven now. Come and sit by the fire and get warm. I'll pour you a drink."

"I don't want a drink."

"Don't you ever drink?"

"My grandmother didn't really approve."

"Your grandmother, if you'll excuse the expression, sounds an old bitch."

Despite herself, Selina smiled. "She wasn't really."

He was surprised by the smile. Still watching it, he said, "What part of London do you live in?"

"Queen's Gate."

"Queen's Gate, S.W.7. And very nice, too. And I suppose your Nanny took you for walks in Kensington Gardens?"

"Yes."

"Do you have brothers and sisters?"

"No."

"Uncles and aunts?"

"No. Nobody."

"No wonder you were so desperately in need of a father."

"I wasn't desperately in need. I just wanted one."

George rocked his glass, watching the tilting amber liq-

uid. He said, "You know, it's occurred to me that people you
. . . are fond of . . . they go on living until some meddle-
some fool comes and tells you they're dead."

Selina said, "I was told years ago that my father was
dead."

"I know, but to-day you've been told for the second time.
And it was I who killed him."

"It wasn't your fault."

"I'm sorry, just the same." He added, more gently, "You
could do with a drink. Just to warm you up."

She shook her head, and he let it go, but it made him feel
uncomfortable just the same. He was so used to being with
Frances, who could hold her own, drink for drink, even if she
did get a little blurry by the end of the evening, and ready to
fight at the drop of a hat; and the next day she was as clear-
headed and bright-eyed as ever, if you could discount the
slight tremor of her hand as she reached out for the tenth
cigarette of the morning.

But this child. He looked at her. Her skin was like ivory,
creamy, quite unflawed. As he watched, she took the towel off
her head and began to rub at her hair to dry it, and her ears
showed, touching, and vulnerable as the back of a baby's neck.

She said, "What are we going to do?"

"What about?"

"About the money. And paying Rudolfo, and getting me
back to London."

"I don't know. I'll have to think about it."

"I could cable my bank in London, and they'd send me
something."

"Yes, you could."

"Would it take long?"

"Three or four days."

"Don't you think, perhaps, I should try and get a room at
the Cala Fuerte Hotel?"

"I doubt if Rudolfo would have you."

87

"I don't really blame him, you know. Even when he was sober, Toni was rather terrifying. Drunk, he must have been really scarey."

"I doubt if he scared Rudolfo."

"Well . . . where am I going to stay?"

"Where else but here? In the *Matrimoniale*. I'd go out to *Eclipse,* only not in this weather, and it won't be the first time I've slept on the sofa."

"If anyone's going to sleep on a sofa, then it should be me."

"Whichever you like. It's all the same to me. I'm sorry that the Casa Barco isn't more conveniently designed, but there's little I can do about it now. I never imagined I'd have a daughter come to stay."

"But I'm not your daughter."

"Then let's say you're George Dyer Junior."

7

Six years ago, when George Dyer had first come to live at Cala Fuerte, Juanita had presented herself at his door and announced, with great dignity, that she would like to work for him. She was the wife of a farmer from San Estaban, she had four children, who were at school in the village, and poverty was never far away. She needed the work, because she needed the money, but there was nothing in her erect and proud demeanour to give any hint of this. She was a small woman, with the square, toiling sturdiness of a working peasant, dark-eyed, short-legged, and with a smile of great charm only spoiled by the fact that she had never cleaned her teeth.

Each morning she was up at half past four, did the daily chores in her own house, fed her family and saw them off to work, and then walked down the hill from San Estaban to Cala Fuerte to present herself at the Casa Barco at half past seven.

She cleaned and cooked for George, did the washing and the ironing, combed the cat and weeded the garden, and was not averse, if the need arose, to taking the dinghy out to *Eclipse* and scrubbing down her decks as well.

When *Fiesta at Cala Fuerte* was published, George gave her a complimentary copy, with a dedication written on the fly-leaf, *"Juanita from George Dyer, with love and respect,"* and it was perhaps her most precious possession, after the marriage bed which had been bequeathed to her by her grandmother, and the linen sheets, heavy as leather, which she had embroidered herself. She spoke no English and read in no language, but the book was already on show in her house, arranged, like an ornament, with a lace doily all to itself. She never let herself into his house. In Juanita's code, this appeared to be a breach of etiquette. Instead, she would sit outside, on the wall, with her hands in her lap and her legs crossed at the ankle, like Royalty, and wait for him to come and open the door and let her in. He would say, *"Buenos días,* Juanita," and they would exchange pleasantries about the weather, and she would ask how the Señor had slept. He had never discovered the reason for this strange shibboleth, and did not like to ask. Perhaps it had something to do with the fact that he did not have a wife.

The morning after the storm he awoke at seven. He had slept on the sofa, after all, because he hadn't the heart to take the comfortable bed for himself. It was very quiet. The wind had died, and when he got up and went to open his shutters and go out on to the terrace, the morning was fresh and quiet as a pearl, without a cloud in the sky, and the world smelt damp and sweet after the rain, although the water of the harbour was murky from the rough weather, and a certain amount of devastation would have to be cleared away. To start with, he picked up his rickety terrace furniture from where it had been ignominiously blown, and tipped a puddle of water from the top of the table, and then he went back inside, and lit a cigarette, and thought that he would make a cup of tea. There was, however, no water in the kettle and he did not like to let the bucket down the well for fear of waking Selina.

He looked for his clothes, but the sweater and pants he had worn last night were unsuitable for the day's work, so he went to the gallery to fetch himself some others. Selina still slept like a child, engulfed by George's pyjamas and the enormous bed. Moving quietly, he took the first shirt and pair of pants that came to hand, and eased himself down the ladder again. He had a shower (the water was icy after the storm) and dressed, and then went to open the door for Juanita. She had not arrived, but if the door stood open, she would come in and start to cook his breakfast. Then he went back out on to the terrace, down the steps to the slipway, pushed out the dinghy and rowed out to *Eclipse*.

She seemed to have weathered the storm with her usual calm. He checked her mooring ropes, then went aboard. With a certain amount of forethought he had secured the tarpaulin cover over the cockpit, and although this sagged with pools of water, the cockpit itself was relatively dry. He loosened off a couple of straining halyards, and went below to make sure that his forward hatches had not let in any of the rain. Reassured, he returned to the cockpit, and perched himself on the coaming and lit a cigarette.

It was going to be a very warm day. Already steam was rising from the wet decks, and the tarpaulin, which he had spread out to dry. The air was so clear that he could see far inland, beyond the distant cross of San Estaban; and so quiet that when a fisherman, busy on his boat, talked in undertones to a companion, George could hear every word. There was only the slightest movement of water. The dinghy's prow resisted this, with a soft lapping sound, but the yacht moved lightly, as though she were breathing.

Soothed by familiar surroundings, familiar smells and sounds, George felt himself begin to unwind. Calmly, now, he

91

could consider the day ahead, and give a certain order to the problems which beset him.

The first was Rudolfo. He did not mind the row; it was not the first and it would not be the last, but Rudolfo was not a wealthy man, and somehow, and soon, the six hundred pesetas had to be paid back. George could not risk waiting until his own money was cleared by the bank in Barcelona. These delays had happened before, and he had once had to wait nearly a month before it came through. If, however, they sent a cable to Selina's bank there was the possibility that the money would be in San Antonio in three or four days, and Rudolfo, knowing this, would be only too pleased to put her up at his hotel, and that way conventions would be respected, and no fine feelings, vulnerable in Cala Fuerte, would be offended.

On the other hand, there was Frances. Frances would lend him six hundred pesetas and Selina's return air fair, if George could bring himself to ask her. But with Frances, money talked. And if he was going to get into her debt, he would not do it for Rudolfo, nor a girl who had come looking for her father, but on his own account, because only he would be able to settle the bill.

A movement from Casa Barco caught his eye, and he looked up and saw that Juanita was on the terrace, hanging the red-and-white blanket from the sofa over the washing line in order to air it. She wore a pink dress and a brown apron, and she went back into the house, only to reappear with a broom, and began to clear up the debris of last night's broken flower-pots.

George wonderd how he was going to explain the presence of Selina in his bed. He had always been very careful never to let such a situation arise, and as far as Juanita was concerned, he had no idea how she might react. He did not like the thought of deceiving her, but on the other hand he did not want to lose her—for any reason. He could tell her the truth, but it was so far-fetched that he doubted whether the simple Juanita would swallow it. Or he could say that Selina was a visiting cousin, who had had to spend the night because of the storm. After some deliberation he decided that this was the best story, and had the added advantage of being more or less true. He tossed his cigarette overboard, let himself down into the dinghy and rowed gently back to Casa Barco.

Juanita was in the galley, boiling a kettle for his coffee

"*Buenos días*, Juanita."

She turned, beaming.

"*Buenos días*, Señor."

He decided to plunge straight in.

"Did you wake the Señorita when you drew the water from the well?"

"No, Señor, she still sleeps, like a baby."

George glanced at Juanita sharply. Her voice was lyrical, her eyes shining with sentiment. This was not exactly what George had expected. He had not even had time to tell his story about the visiting cousin, and here was Juanita already looking all dewy-eyed . . . about what?

"You've . . . been up to see her then . . . ?"

"*Sí*, Señor, I went to see if she was awake. But, Señor," her voice dropped to a tone of mild reproach, "why did you never tell me that you had a daughter?"

George felt behind him for the arm of the sofa, and sat on it. "I never told you?" he said, stupidly.

"No, you have said no word about your daughter. And when Maria tells me, this morning, as I come through Cala Fuerte, that the Señor's daughter is staying at the Casa Barco, I would not believe it. But it is true."

George swallowed, and said, with forced calm, "Maria told you. And who told Maria?"

"Tomeu has told her."

"Tomeu?"

"*Sí*, Señor. There was a taxi-driver who brought her here. He spent many hours in the bar of Rudolfo, and he told Rosita,

93

who works there, that he had taken the daughter of Señor Dyer to the Casa Barco. Rosita told Tomeu when she went to buy some soap powder, and Tomeu told Maria, and Maria told Juanita."

"And the rest of the village, I'll be bound," George muttered, in English, and silently cursed Selina.

"Señor?"

"It is nothing, Juanita."

"Are you not pleased to have your daughter?"

"Yes, of course."

"I did not know that the Señor had been married."

George thought for a second and then said, "Her mother is dead."

Juanita was devastated. "Señor, I did not know. And who has taken care of the Señorita?"

"Her grandmother," said George, wondering how much longer he was going to get away from telling the truth. "Juanita, tell me . . . does Rudolfo know that . . . the Señorita is my daughter?"

"I have not seen Rudolfo, Señor."

The kettle boiled, and she filled the earthenware jug that George had taught her to keep for coffee. The smell was delicious, but did nothing to cheer him. Juanita put the lid on the coffee-pot and said, "Señor, she is very beautiful."

"Beautiful?" He sounded amazed, because he was.

"But of course she is beautiful." Juanita carried his breakfast tray past him and out on to the terrace. "The Señor does not have to pretend with me."

He ate his breakfast. An orange, a sweet *ensamada,* and as much coffee as the pot contained. Juanita moved about inside the house, soft-footed and making gentle sweeping sounds which indicated that she was cleaning. Presently she emerged with the round washing-basket, filled with clothes.

He said, "The Señorita got very wet last night, in the

storm, and I told her to put her clothes on the floor of the bathroom."

"*Sí*, Señor, I have found them."

"Do them quickly as you can, Juanita. She has nothing else to wear."

"*Sí*, Señor."

She went past him and down the steps to her little cave of a wash-house, where she scrubbed sheets, socks and shirts impartially, boiling water in a great tub and using a bar of soap as large and as hard as a brick.

The first thing to do was go and see Rudolfo. As George went through the house, he glanced up at the gallery but there was no movement and not a sound. He cursed his visitor silently, but left her sleeping, and went out, and because he could not be bothered to open the garage doors and start up his car, began to walk to the village.

He was to regret this. For, before he had reached the Cala Fuerte Hotel, no fewer than seven people had congratulated him on having his daughter come to stay with him. As each encounter took place, George walked a little faster, as though on some errand of desperate urgency, giving the impression that much as he would like to stop and discuss this new and happy state of affairs, he simply did not have the time. Consequently he arrived at Rudolfo's bar, out of breath and soaked in sweat, and feeling as if he had been caught in a trap. He stood in the curtained doorway, panting with exhaustion, and said, "Rudolfo. Am I allowed in?"

Rudolfo was behind the bar, polishing glasses. When he saw George, his hands were still. His smile began to spread. "George, my friend." He laid down the glass and came out from behind the bar as if to embrace George.

George eyed him warily. "You're not going to hit me?"

"It is you who should be hitting me. But I did not know. I was only told, this morning, by Rosita, that the Señorita is your daughter. Why did you not tell me last night? That she was your child. I did not even know that you had a child. And so beautiful . . ."

"Rudolfo, there's been a mistake. . . ."

"And it was my mistake. And what kind of a man must you think I am, to grudge a favour to an old friend and his child?"

"But . . ."

Rudolfo raised a hand. "There can be no buts. Six hundred pesetas, well," he shrugged, "it doesn't grow on trees, but it will not ruin me."

"Rudolfo . . ."

"My friend, if you say more I shall think that you have not forgiven me. Come, let us have a drink together—a cognac. . . ."

It was impossible. He refused to listen to the truth and George was not going to push it down his throat. He said weakly, "I'd rather have a coffee," and Rudolfo went to shout for it and George hitched himself on to one of the bar stools and lit a cigarette. When Rudolfo returned he said, "You'll get your money back. We can cable to London . . ."

"You will have to go to San Antonio to send a cable."

"Well, fair enough. How long would you reckon it would take to come?"

Rudolfo shrugged hugely. "Two or three days. Maybe a week. It's of no importance. I can wait a week for six hundred pesetas."

"You're a good man, Rudolfo."

"But I get angry. You know I get angry."

"You're still a good man."

The coffee came, brought by Rosita, the unconscious source of the trouble. George watched her set down the minuscule cups and told himself that he was deeper in deception than ever. And he realised, with a slight sinking of his heart, that there was now no need to ask his second favour of

Rudolfo. If Selina was to be George's daughter, there could be no point in her coming to live at the Cala Fuerte Hotel.

It was Pearl who woke Selina. She had been out all night, was tired from hunting and in need of a soft place to sleep. She came into the Casa Barco by way of the terrace, trod lightly up the stair to the gallery, and jumped, with scarcely a sound, on to the bed. Selina opened her eyes and looked straight into Pearl's white, whiskered face. Pearl's eyes were jade-green, the dark pupils mere slits of contentment. She trod the sheets for a little, making a nest, then fitted her boneless, furry body into the curve of Selina's own and proceeded to go to sleep.

Selina rolled over and did the same thing.

The second time she was awakened more roughly. "Come on, now, it's time to wake up. It's eleven o'clock. Come on, now." She was being shaken, and when she opened her eyes, George Dyer was sitting on the side of the bed. "It's time you woke up," he said again.

"Umm?" The cat was still there, deliciously heavy and warm. George, once focused, loomed enormous. He wore a blue cotton shirt and a grim expression, and Selina's heart sank. She was never at her best first thing in the morning.

"It's time you woke up."

"What time is it?"

"I told you. Nearly eleven. I've got to talk to you."

"Oh." She pulled herself up and searched for pillows that had disappeared. George stooped to pick them up off the floor, and shoved them behind her. "Now, listen," he said. "I've been to see Rudolfo . . ."

"Is he still angry?"

"No, he's not angry. Not any more. You see, Rudolfo, and for that matter the entire village, believe that you really are my daughter. You know why they think that, don't you? Because your drunken taxi-driver, damn his eyes, told them so."

"Oh," said Selina.

"Yes. Oh. *Did* you tell the taxi-driver I was your father."

"Yes," she admitted.

"For God's sake why?"

"I had to, to make him bring me here. I said, 'My father will pay the taxi fare,' and that was the only thing that persuaded him."

"You had no right to do that. To involve an innocent party . . ."

"You?"

"Yes, me. I'm up to my neck in this now."

"I never thought he would tell all the village."

"He didn't. He told Rosita, the girl who works in Rudolfo's bar. And Rosita told Tomeu. And Tomeu told his mother. And Maria is the Official Receiving and Transmitting Station for this part of the island."

"I see," said Selina. "I am sorry. But can't we tell them the truth?"

"Not now."

"Why not now?"

"Because the people here . . ." he chose his words carefully, "have a very rigid standard of morals."

"Then why did you let me stay last night?"

He was exasperated. "Because of the storm. Because of the row with Rudolfo. Because there wasn't any alternative."

"And you've said that I am your daughter?"

"I haven't said that you're not."

"But you're much too young. We worked it out last night."

"No one else is to know that."

"But it's not true."

"It wasn't true when you told the taxi-driver."

"Yes, but I didn't *know* it wasn't true!"

"And I do. Is that it? Well, I'm sorry if your principles are offended, but these people are my friends and I don't want to disillusion them. Not that they have many illusions about me, but at least they don't think I'm a liar."

She still looked troubled, so he changed the subject.
"Now, about this money. You say that we can cable to your
bank . . ."

"Yes."

"But not from Cala Fuerte. We have to go into San Antonio to send a cable. We can either send a wire directly to your
bank, or it occurred to me on the way home, we might get in
touch with your lawyer . . ."

"Oh, no," said Selina, with such vehemence that George
raised his eyebrows in surprise.

"Why not?"

"Let's just cable the bank."

"But your lawyer would be able to get the money through
so much more quickly."

"I don't want to cable Rodney."

"Don't you like him?"

"It isn't that. It's just that . . . well, he thought this
whole business of coming to find my father was crazy."

"As things have turned out, he wasn't far wrong."

"I don't want him to know what a fiasco it's all been. Try
to understand."

"Well, sure I understand, but if it meant the money coming through more quickly . . ." Her face remained resolutely
stubborn, and George, suddenly fed up with the whole business, stopped trying to persuade her. "Well, all right. It's your
money and your time. And your reputation."

Selina ignored this. "Do you want to go to San Antonio to-
day?"

"Soon as you can be up and dressed. Are you feeling hungry?"

"Not particularly."

"How about a cup of coffee?"

"If there's one going."

"I'll make you one."

99

He was half-way down the ladder when she called him back.

"Mr. Dyer . . ."

He turned, only his top half visible.

Selina said, "I haven't got anything to put on."

"I'll speak to Juanita."

He found her on the terrace, ironing, with the flex of the iron trailing through the open window.

"Juanita."

"Señor."

"The Señorita's things? Are they ready?"

"Sí, Señor." She beamed, delighted with her own efficiency, and handed him a pile of neatly-folded clothes. He thanked her, and went back into the house, to meet Selina coming down the steps from the gallery. Still in his pyjamas, she looked tousled and sleepy. He said, "Here," and handed her the pile.

"Oh, how wonderful!"

"Just one of the services in this hotel."

"She's been so quick . . . I never thought . . ." The words tailed to a stop. George frowned. From the top of the pile of clothes, Selina took her dress. Or what remained of it. Juanita had treated the good British wool just as she treated the rest of her washing. With hot water, hard soap and much scrubbing. Selina held it out at arm's length. It might have fitted a very small six-year-old and the only thing that rendered it recognisable was the silk Fortnum and Mason label on the inside of the collar.

There was a long silence. Then George said, "It's a Little Brown Dress."

"She's washed it! Why did she have to wash it? It didn't need to be washed; it was only wet. . . ."

"If it's anyone's fault, it's mine. I told Juanita to wash it, and if I tell Juanita to do a thing, she certainly does it." He began to laugh.

"I don't think it's anything to laugh about. It's all very well for you to laugh, but what am I going to wear?"

"What is there to do except laugh?"

"I could cry."

"That won't do any good."

"I can't wear pyjamas all day long."

"Why not? They're very fetching."

"I can't come to San Antonio in pyjamas."

Still enormously amused, but trying to be sensible, George scratched the back of his head. "What about your coat?"

"I should die of heat in my coat. Oh, why do all these horrible, horrible things have to happen?"

He tried to soothe her. "Now look . . ."

"No, I *won't* look!"

It was a typical example of the blind injustice of arguing with a woman, and George lost patience.

"All right then, don't look. Go and jump on the bed and cry for the rest of the day, but before you do, come and help me compose a cable to send to your bank. I'll take it into San Antonio myself, and you can stay here and sulk."

"That's the most horrible, unfair thing to say . . ."

"All right, Junior, so it's horrible. Maybe I say horrible things because I'm a horrible person. It's as well you found out in good time. Now, come and sit down and put that pin-brain of yours into action and let's get this cable written."

"I have not got a pin-brain," Selina defended herself. "And even if I had, you haven't known me long enough to find out. All I'm saying is that I can't walk round in my under-clothes all day. . . ."

"Look, this is Cala Fuerte San Antonio, not Queen's Gate, S.W.7. Personally, I don't care if you walk around stark naked, but I'd prefer to get hold of that money as soon as possible, and return you, unopened, as it were, to Kensington Gardens and Nanny." He was leaning over his desk, finding a clean sheet of paper and a pencil, but now he looked up, his brown eyes unreadable, and said, "If you were older and more experienced, I rather think you'd have slapped my face by now."

Selina told herself that if she cried, in rage, or for any other reason, she would never forgive herself. She said in a voice that shook only slightly, "The idea never entered my head."

"Good. Don't let it." He sat down at the desk and drew the sheet of paper towards him. "Now, the name of your bank . . ."

8

After the quiet, tree-shaded cool of Cala Fuerte, San Antonio that afternoon seemed hot and dusty and inordinately full. The streets were packed with traffic. Hooting cars and motor scooters, wooden donkey carts and bicycles. The narrow pavements were so crowded that pedestrians, careless of life, overflowed into the road, and George found that it was impossible to make any sort of progress without the heel of his hand more or less permanently on the horn.

The cable office and his own bank were both situated in the main plaza of the town, facing each other across the tree-lined walks and the fountains. George parked his car in a shady spot, lit a cigarette, and went, first, into the bank to see if by any chance his own money had come through from Barcelona. If it had, he planned to collect the lot in cash, tear up Selina's cable, and go then and there to the airport and buy her return ticket to London.

But the money had still not come. The cashier suggested kindly that if George would like to sit and wait for perhaps four or five hours, he would endeavour to get through to Barcelona and find out what had happened. George, in fascinated interest, asked why he would have to wait four or five hours, only to be told that the telephone was broken and had not yet been repaired.

After six years of living in the island, he was still torn between exasperation and amusement at the local attitude to time, but he said that it didn't matter, he would do without the money, and he went out of the bank, and across the square, and up the impressive stairway to the soaring marble halls of the cable office.

He copied the message out on to an official form, and then joined a slow-moving shuffling queue. When at last he reached the wire grille and it was his turn, his patience was running short. The man behind the grille had a polished brown head and a wart on his nose and spoke no English. It took him a long time to read the message, to count the words, and consult manuals. Eventually he stamped the form, and told George that it would cost ninety-five pesetas.

George paid him. "When will it get to London?"

The man eyed the clock. "To-night . . . maybe."

"You'll send it off right away?"

The wart-nosed man did not deign to reply. He looked over George's shoulder. "Next, please."

There was nothing more to be done. He went back outside, lit another cigarette, and debated on his next move. In the end he decided that it would be worth going to the Yacht Club to pick up his mail, but not worth taking the car. He started to walk.

The crowds made him feel claustrophobic. He stayed in the middle of the streets, stepping aside every now and then to let the motor traffic brush by. Overhead, small balconies bulged with humanity. Enormous, black-clad grannies sat with their embroidery, enjoying the spring sunshine. Clusters of children, their eyes like grapes, peered through the wrought-iron lace of the railings, and washing, like celebration bunting, zig-zagged from one side of the street to the other, and over all was the San Antonio smell. Of drains and fish, and cedar wood and Ideales cigarettes, overlaid with unidentifiable harbour smells that blew in from the sea.

He came to a small cross-roads and stopped on the edge of the pavement, waiting for the traffic to clear so that he could cross. A cripple, in a little booth, sold lottery tickets, and on the corner of the block was a shop, the window filled with embroidered blouses and cotton dresses and beach hats and shoes and bathing-suits.

George thought of Selina. He told himself that he could not wait to put her on the London plane, and to be rid of her, but she wouldn't be able to travel if she didn't have a dress to wear. Perhaps he should buy her a dress. But even as he went in through the door, he was visited by a second and far more amusing idea.

"*Buenos días*, Señor," said the red-headed woman, getting up from behind her small glass counter.

"*Buenos días*," said George, and, straight-faced, he told her what he wanted.

Five minutes later he was back in the crowded streets, carrying the little parcel wrapped so carefully in pink-and-white-striped paper. He was still grinning to himself, when the car horn blared behind him. He swore and stepped aside and the long black snout of a Citröen brushed alongside the seat of his pants, and stopped.

"Well," said an unmistakable voice. "Look who just rode into town."

It was Frances. She sat in her open car, looking both surprised and pleased. She wore sun-glasses and a man's straw hat tipped over her nose and a faded pink shirt. She leaned across to open the door. "Hop in and I'll take you some place."

He got in beside her, and the leather upholstery was so hot that he felt as if he were being grilled, but before he had even shut the door Frances had moved forward again, slowly, nosing through the crowds.

She said, "I didn't expect to see you back so soon."

"I didn't expect to be here."

"How long have you been in?"

"Half an hour or so. I had to send a cable."

Frances did not comment on this. Another cluster of pedestrians had gathered ahead. Fat ladies in cotton dresses and white cardigans, with very new straw hats and painfully sun-burned faces. Frances's horn blared again, and they looked up, surprised, from the postcards they had been buying, and backed unresentfully up on to the already bursting pavements.

"Where the hell have they all come from?" George wanted to know.

"It's a cruise ship in. The first of the season."

"Oh, God, has it started already?"

Frances shrugged. "You have to make the best of it. At least it brings cash into the town." She glanced down at the little parcel in his lap. "What have you been buying at Teresa's shop?"

"How do you know it was Teresa's shop?"

"The pink-and-white-striped paper. I'm intrigued."

George thought for a moment. He said, "It's handker-chiefs."

"Didn't know you used them." They had come to the main street of the town, an artery of traffic controlled by a wickedly-tempered Guardia Civil. The Citröen moved down into second gear, and Frances said, "Where'd you want to go?"

"There might be some mail at the Yacht Club."

"Didn't you pick it up yesterday?"

"Yes, but there might be some more."

She glanced at him sideways. "Did you get home all right?"

"Sure."

"Boat O.K.?"

"Yes, she's all right. Did you get that second storm yesterday evening?"

"No, it missed us."

"You were lucky. It was a corker."

They waited at the traffic lights until the red changed to green, then Frances turned down a narrow street and on to the broad harbour road. This was George's favourite part of San Antonio, packed with cheerful little waterfront bars, and ships' chandlers, smelling of tar and grain and paraffin. The harbour was filled with craft. Island schooners, and yachts, and the Barcelona boat, getting steam up to sail, and the cruise ship, from Bremen, tied up at the north pier.

He saw a strange yacht, new since yesterday. He said, "She's flying a Dutch flag."

"A young people called Van Trikker, doing a circumnavigation." Frances made it her business to find these things out.

"Through the Mediterranean?"

"Well, why not? That's what the Suez Canal is for."

He grinned. Frances leaned forward and took a pack of cigarettes out of the dashboard shelf and handed it to him, and he took it and lit one for himself and one for her. When they got to the Yacht Club, he went inside for his mail, and Frances sat and waited for him, and when he returned with two letters stuffed in the back pocket of his pants, she said, "Where now?"

"I'm going to have a drink."

"I'll come with you."

"Oughtn't you to be selling original Olaf Svensens to all those lovely tourists?"

107

"I have a young student working for me. She can take care of the Germans." She turned the car in a single sweep. "I'd much rather take care of you."

They went to Pedro's, a little way along the road. Pedro had pulled some tables and chairs out on to the wide pavement, and they sat in the shade of a tree, and George ordered a beer for himself and cognac for Frances.

She said, "Daring, you're very abstemious all of a sudden."

"I have a genuine thirst."

"I hope it isn't painful."

She reached around his back for the letters he had stuffed in his pocket and laid them on the table in front of him and said, "Open them."

"Why?"

"Because I'm curious. I like to know what's in letters, especially other people's. I don't like to think of them ageing gracefully, like well-bred old ladies. Here. . . ." She picked a knife off the carelessly-laid table, and slit the flaps of the envelopes. "Now all you have to do is take them out and read them."

Humouring her, George did so. The first contained a letter from a yachting magazine to say that they would pay him eight pounds ten shillings for an article he had submitted to them.

He handed this over to Frances and she read it, and said, "There, what did I tell you? Good news."

"Better than nothing." He took out the second letter.

"What was the article about?"

"Self-steering gears."

She patted his back. "Well, aren't you a clever boy. . . . Who's that one from?"

It was from his publisher, but he was reading the letter, and did not hear the question.

George Dyer, Esq.,
Club Nautica,
San Antonio,
Baleares,
Spain.

Dear Mr. Dyer,

I have written you no fewer than five letters over the last four months in the hope that you would be able to let us have at least some sort of synopsis for a second book as a follow-up to *Fiesta at Cala Fuerte*. I have not had a rely to any of them. All these letters were addressed to the Club Nautica at San Antonio, and I am now wondering whether perhaps this is no longer your Poste Restante.

As I pointed out when we agreed to publish *Fiesta at Cala Fuerte*, a follow-up is important if we are to maintain the public's interest in you as a writer. *Cala Fuerte* has sold well and is into its third printing, and negotiations are under way for a paperback; but we must have a second book from you soon, if your sales are not to deteriorate.

It is unfortunate that we were unable to meet personally and discuss this matter, but I think I made it clear when we agreed to publish *Fiesta at Cala Fuerte* that we could only do it on condition that it would be the first of a series, and I was under the impression that you understood this.

In any event, I should be grateful for a reply to this letter.

Yours sincerely,
ARTHUR RUTLAND

He read this through twice and then dropped it on the table. The waiter had brought their drinks, and the beer was so cold that it frosted the tall glass, and when he put his hand around it it was an actual pain, like touching ice.

Frances said, "Who's it from?"

"Read it."

"I don't want to read it if you'd rather I didn't."

"Oh, read the thing."

She did so, and he drank his beer.

She reached the bottom of the page, and said, "Well, I think that's the hell of a letter. Who does he think he is?"

"My publisher."

"For heaven's sake, you're under no contract!"

"Publishers don't like one-book men, Frances. They want either nothing at all, or a good steady stream."

"He's written to you before?"

"Yes, of course he has. He's been on at me for the last four or five months. That's why I've given up opening my letters."

"Have you *tried* to write a second book?"

"Tried? I've ruptured myself trying. What the hell am I to write it about? I only wrote the first one because I thought I was running out of money, and it was a long, chilly winter. I never thought I'd get it published."

"But you've been around, George . . . you've done so many things. That cruise in the Aegean . . ."

"Do you think I didn't try to write about that? I spent three weeks bashing words on to my typewriter, and it was as dull to read as it had been to write. Anyway it's been done before. Everything's been done before."

Frances took a final drag of her cigarette, and then stubbed it out, carefully, in the ash-tray. Her brown hands were as big as a man's, the nails very large and painted bright red. She wore a heavy gold bracelet and as she moved her arm, it clashed on the wood of the table. She said, carefully, "Is it really that much of a disaster? After all, you've had one successful book, and if you can't write a second, then you just can't."

A boat was moving out of the yacht club basin. Across the water came the rattle of shackles, and the sail slid up the mast. It hung slack for a moment, and then the boy at the tiller moved the boat around and the sail shivered slightly and shook out its folds and swelled into a smooth, strong curve, and the boat heeled over and ran forward, and was pulled closer to the wind and heeled some more.

He said, "I don't like to break a promise."

"Oh, darling, you talk as if it were a personal thing."

"Isn't it?"

"No, it's business."

"Would you break a business promise, just like that?"

"Of course not. But writing isn't like selling stocks, or doing accounts. It's creative and it doesn't work with the same set of rules. If you have a writer's block, then there's nothing you can do."

"Writer's block," said George bitterly. "Is that what it's called?"

She laid her hand on his arm, heavy with the weight of the bracelet. "Why don't you forget about it? Write to Mr. . . ." she glanced at the signature on the letter, "Rutland, and say, Well, O.K. if that's how you feel, to hell with any more books."

"You really think I could do that, don't you. And what then?"

She shrugged. "Well . . ." Her voice began to drawl. "There are other diversions."

"Such as."

"In two weeks it'll be Easter." She picked up the knife she had used to slit his envelopes, and began tracing the grain of the table with its tip. "I've been asked to Malagar for the Easter Sunday *corrida*. I have friends there, Americans. They are great *aficionados*. At Malagar you get the best bulls and the best *toreros* in Spain. And there are parties all day long and all night long."

111

"It sounds like a travel agent's dream."

"Darling, don't get sour with me. I didn't write that letter, I just read it."

"I know, I'm sorry."

"Will you come with me? To Malagar."

The waiter was hovering. George called him over and paid for the drinks and the boy took away the glasses and George gave him a tip, and when the boy had gone, he gathered up his cap and the pink-and-white-striped parcel and his two letters.

Frances said, "You haven't answered my question."

He stood up, holding the back of his chair.

"I think you've forgotten that I was never an *aficianado*. The sight of blood makes me faint."

She said, like a child, "I want you to be there. . . ."

"I'd spoil it all."

She looked away, trying not to show her disappointment. She said, "Where are you going now?"

"Back to Cala Fuerte."

"Can't you stay here?"

"No, I must get back."

"Don't tell me you have to feed that cat again."

"I have more things to feed than the cat." He touched her shoulder in farewell. "Thanks for the ride."

Darkness fell as George drove back to Cala Fuerte. Once the sun had slipped out of the sky, the air became chill, and at dusk he stopped by a lonely farmhouse and reached for the spare sweater he had brought with him. As his head emerged from the neck of the sweater, he saw the farmer's wife come out of her house to draw water from the well. The open door glowed with yellow light and she was silhouetted against it, and he called *"Buenas tardes"* to her and she came over to chat for a little, resting her water-jug against her hip and asking him where he had been and where he was going.

He was thirsty, so he took a drink of water from her, and then went on his way, his headlights probing the sapphire evening. The first stars began to prick the sky and San Estaban was a saucer of lights in the shadow of the mountain, and as he came down the last stretch of the road towards Cala Fuerte, the wind blew off the sea and brought with it the fresh resinous smell of the pines.

Unaccountably, but inevitably, this feeling of coming home always cheered him up. Now, his spirits lifted, and he realised how depressed and tired he had been feeling all day. Nothing, much, had gone right. The letter from Mr. Rutland was an added weight to his conscience, and he was still saddled with Miss Queen's Gate. He wondered how she had spent her day, and told himself that he did not particularly care, but he could not help hoping, as he bowled down the last slope of the road towards the Casa Barco, that she would not still be in a sulk.

He put the car in the garage, turned off the engine, glanced at his watch. It was past eight o'clock. He got out of the car and crossed the lane and opened the door of the Casa Barco, and went in. There did not seem to be anybody about, although the house bore witness to a certain amount of unaccustomed care and attention. The fire was blazing, the lamps lighted, and the low coffee table by the hearth laid with a blue-and-white cloth, which George had not known he possessed, and knives and forks and glasses. There was also a bowl of wild flowers and the air was filled with the delicious smell of cooking. He laid down his cap and went out on to the terrace, soft-footed in his rope-soled shoes, but the terrace was dark and there was no sign of his guest. He went to lean over the wall, but the slipways were empty, the only sound was the whisper of water and the creak as his dinghy tugged at her mooring. Then, from one of the harbour cafés came the warm chords of a guitar, and a woman started to sing, the strange two-tone warbling that was one of the Moorish legacies of the island.

He frowned, puzzled, and went back into the house. The gallery was in darkness, but the light was on in the kitchen, and when he went to lean over the counter, he was surprised to find Selina squatting in front of the open oven, basting a casserole with enormous concentration.

He said, to the top of her head, "Good evening."

Selina looked up. He had not startled her, and he realised that she had known all along that he was there, and he found this disconcerting. It seemed to give her some sort of advantage.

She said, "Hello!"

"What are you doing?"

"Cooking dinner."

"Smells good."

"I hope it is. I'm not much good at cooking, I'm afraid."

"What is it?"

"Steak and onions and peppers and things."

"I didn't think we had any food in the house."

"We didn't. I went up to Maria's and bought it."

"You did?" He was impressed. "But Maria doesn't talk any English."

"No, I know. But I found a dictionary in the drawer in your desk."

"What did you use for money?"

"I'm afraid I put it down on your account. I bought myself a pair of espadrilles, too. They were eight pesetas. I hope you don't mind."

"Not at all."

She eyed the casserole critically. "Do you think it looks all right?"

"It looks splendid."

"I did think I'd roast the meat, but I couldn't find any fat except olive oil, and somehow I didn't think that would work."

She picked up a towel, put the lid back on the casserole, and returned the whole fragrant dish back into the oven. She closed the door and stood up. They faced each other over the counter and she said, "Did you have a good day?"

In the light of all this domesticity, George had forgotten about his day. "What . . . oh, yes. Yes, all right."

"Did you get the cable off?"

"Yes. Yes, I sent the cable." She had some freckles on her nose, and under the light her smooth hair shone with unexpected streaks of fairness.

"How long did they say it would take?"

"Just what we thought. Three or four days." He leaned on his crossed forearms, and said, "And how did you fill in the day?"

"Oh . . ." She seemed nervous, and for something to do with her hands, wiped at the top of the counter with the cloth she was still holding, like a diligent barmaid. "Well, I made friends with Juanita, and I washed my hair and I sat on the terrace in the sun . . ."

"You have freckles."

"Yes, I know. Isn't it awful. And then I went up to the village to do the shopping and that took me ages, because everybody wanted to talk to me and of course I couldn't understand a word they said. And then I came back and peeled some vegetables . . ."

"And lit the fire . . ." George interrupted. "And did some flowers . . ."

"You noticed! They'll be dead to-morrow, they're just wild; I picked them on the way back from the village." He did not comment on this, and she went on, quickly, as though nervous of any lull in the conversation, "Have you had anything to eat to-day?"

"No, I skipped lunch. I had a glass of beer at four."

"Are you hungry?"

"Ravenous."

"I just have to make a salad. It'll be ready in about ten minutes."

115

"Are you hinting that I should go and put on a dinner jacket and my bow tie?"

"No, I'm not doing anything of the sort."

He grinned at her, straightened up and stretched. "I'll make a bargain with you," he said. "I'll go and wash the dust out of my ears and you can pour me a drink."

She looked doubtful. "What sort of a drink?"

"A Scotch and soda. With ice."

"I wouldn't know how much whisky to put in."

"Two fingers." He showed her how to measure. "Well, maybe three of your fingers. Got the idea?"

"I can always try."

"Good girl. You do that."

He collected a clean shirt and took a swift and icy shower and had dressed again and was combing his hair when his reflection told him that he needed a shave.

George squared up to his reflection and told it, without mincing words, that he needed that drink far more.

The reflection acquired a sanctimonious inner voice. *If she can lay a table and be bothered to pick a bunch of flowers you can surely shave.*

I never asked her to pick the bloody flowers.

You never asked her to cook the dinner either, but you're going to eat it.

Oh, shut up! said George, and reached for his razor.

He did it in style, finishing off with the remains of some after-shave which had been so little used that it had started to congeal in the bottom of the bottle.

Oh, very nice, his reflection said now, standing back to admire him.

Satisfied? George asked, and his reflection gave him a sardonic grin.

The whisky was waiting for him, on the table by the fire, but Selina had gone back to the kitchen, and was tossing a salad in his big wooden bowl. He picked up his transistor and went to sit with his back to the fire, and tried to find some music they could listen to, and Selina said, "They're having some sort of a party down on the harbour. You can hear the singing."

"I know; it's riveting, isn't it?"

"It doesn't sound like a proper tune."

"It wouldn't. It's Moorish."

The transistor, from squeaks and warblings, moved into warm guitar music. George laid it down, and picked up his glass, and Selina said, "I hope your drink's all right."

He tried it. It was too strong. He said, "Perfect."

"I only hope the dinner's perfect, too. I should have bought some fresh bread at Maria's as well, but there seemed to be masses of bread, so I didn't."

"Juanita is a secret bread addict. She has it for elevenses every day with goat's cheese and a tumbler of *vino tinto*. How she keeps awake, I don't know."

Selina picked up the salad bowl and came out from behind the counter to put it in the middle of the laid table. She was wearing a blue-and-green-striped shirt which George had never liked till now, and a pair of navy-blue pants, very neat and trim, and belted around her waist with a narrow strip of leather. He had genuinely forgotten what their row this morning had been about; the whole ridiculous business had gone clean out of his mind, but now his subconscious did a swift double-take, and he recognised the belt as one of his own, and as she moved away from him, back towards the galley, he reached out and took hold of it.

He said, "Where did you get those pants?"

Selina, held like a puppy by its tail, said, "They're yours."

Her casual tone was not convincing. "They're *mine*?" They were, too. They were his best navy-blue serge pants. He set down his glass and turned her to face him. "But they fit you." She met his eyes, but only just. "What have you done to my best trousers?"

117

"Well . . ." Her eyes widened. "You know, when you'd gone this morning, well, I didn't have anything much to do so I was tidying around and I noticed, well, that these trousers you had on last night were rather dirty. I mean, there were marks down the side of the leg, like gravy or something. So I took them down and showed them to Juanita, and Juanita washed them for you. And they shrank."

After this outrageous fabrication, she had the grace to look a little embarrassed. George said, "That is a flaming lie, and you know it. Those trousers had just come back from the cleaners, and ever since *I* got back from San Antonio, you've been looking like a cat with two tails. And I, poor mistaken fool, imagined it was because you'd been clever and cooked poor old George a good dinner. But it wasn't, was it?"

Selina said, plaintively, "But I didn't have *anything* to wear."

"So you took your revenge on my best pants."

"It wasn't revenge."

"Just because you can't take a joke against yourself."

"Well, you don't seem to be taking this one very well."

"This is different."

"How different?"

He glared at her, but already he realised that his initial rage was wearing thin, and the humour of the situation was getting the better of him. Also, there was a gleam in Selina's eye which suggested an entirely unsuspected side to her character. He said, "I never thought you'd have the guts to stand up for yourself."

"Is that why you're angry . . . ?"

"No, of course it isn't. I'm glad you've got guts. And anyway," he added, remembering delightedly that he could cap the dirty trick she had played on him. "I have something to give you."

"You do?"

"Yes." He had thrown the parcel down with his cap and

now went to retrieve it. "I bought you a present in San Antonio. I hope you like it."

She looked at the tiny package doubtfully. "It couldn't be anything to wear . . ."

"Open it and see," said George, picking up his drink again.

She did, meticulously untying the knots in the string. The paper fell away, and she held up the two halves of the minute pink gingham bikini he had bought her.

He said, very seriously, "You seemed so upset this morning, about having nothing to wear. I do hope the colour will suit you."

Selina could think of nothing to say. The bikini seemed to her to be both suggestive and shocking. That she had been given it by George Dyer made the situation too embarrassing for words. He surely wouldn't imagine that she could ever put it on?

Blushing, not looking at him, she managed to say, "Thank you."

He began to laugh. She glanced up, frowning, and he said, quiet gently, "Did nobody ever tease you before?"

Selina felt a fool. She shook her head.

"Not even Nanny?" He put on a ridiculous voice, and at once it was not embarrassing any longer, but funny.

"Oh, be quiet about Nanny," said Selina, but his amusement was as catching as the measles, and he said, "Don't try to stop smiling. You should smile all the time. You're really very pretty when you smile."

119

9

At half past seven the next morning, George Dyer opened his door to Juanita, and found her, as usual, sitting on the wall with her hands in her lap and a basket at her feet. The basket was covered with a clean white cloth, and Juanita beamed self-consciously as she picked it up and came into the house.

George said, "Now what have you got in there, Juanita?"

"It is a present for the Señorita. Some oranges from the tree of Pepe, Maria's husband."

"Did Maria send them?"

"Sí, Señor."

"That was kind."

"The Señorita is still asleep?"

"I think so. I haven't been to look."

While Juanita was drawing water to make his coffee, he opened the shutters and let the morning into the house. He went out on to the terrace and the stone floor was cool beneath his feet. *Eclipse* lay quietly, her crosstrees white against the pines of the far shore. He decided that perhaps, to-day, he would take out the new propeller. Otherwise there was nothing that he had to do. The day stretched ahead of him, blissfully empty, to use as he chose. He looked up, and thought that the sky looked good. There was a certain amount of cloud inland, beyond San Estaban, but rain always gathered around the high peaks of the mountains, and out to sea it was clear and cloudless.

The clangour of the bucket as it went down the well had wakened Selina, and presently she joined George, wearing the shirt she had borrowed last night, and apparently not much else. Her long, slender legs were not pale any more, but tanned lightly to the colour of a fresh egg, and she had bundled up her hair into an ingenuous knot from which trailed one or two long strands. She came to lean over the terrace wall beside him, and he saw the thin gold chain which she wore around her neck and which doubtless supported a childhood locket, or a gold Confirmation cross. He had always disliked the word innocence, associating it as he did, with fat, pink babies and shiny postcards of winsome kittens; but now, unbidden, it sprang to his mind, as clear and unmistakable as the chime of a bell.

She was watching Pearl, who performed her morning ablutions in a small patch of sun on the slipway below them. Every now and then a fish would dart in the shallows, and Pearl would stop washing herself and freeze to stillness, back leg erect as a lamp-post, only to return to the business in hand.

Selina said, "The day Tomeu brought us to the Casa Barco, there were two fishermen down there, cleaning fish, and Tomeu talked to them."

"That was Rafael, Tomeu's cousin. He keeps his boat in the pen next to mine."

"Are all the village related to each other?"

121

"More or less. Juanita has brought you a present."

She turned to look at him, her escaping strands of hair hanging down like tassels. "She has? What is it?"

"Go and see."

"I already said good morning to her, but she didn't say anything about a present."

"That's because she doesn't speak English. Go on in, she's longing to give it to you."

Selina disappeared into the house. A strange exchange of conversation could be overheard, and presently she reappeared, carrying the basket with the cloth off the top.

"Oranges."

"*Las naranjas,*" said George.

"Is that what they're called? I think she said they were from Maria."

"Maria's husband grew them himself."

"Wasn't that kind?"

"You'll have to go up and thank her."

"I can't do anything unless I learn to speak Spanish. How long did you take to learn?"

He shrugged. "Four months. Living here. I didn't speak a word before that."

"But French."

"Oh, yes, French. And a little Italian. Italian is a great help."

"I must try to learn just a few words."

"I have a grammar I'll lend you, and then you can mug up some verbs as well."

"I know *Buenos días* is good morning . . ."

"And *Buenas tardes* is good afternoon, and *Buenas noches* is good night."

"And *Sí.* I know that. *Sí* is yes."

"And *No* is no, which is a much more important word for a young girl to learn."

"Even I, with my pin-brain, can remember that one."

"Oh, I wouldn't be too sure."

Juanita came out with the breakfast tray and began to lay the cups and plates and the coffee things out on the table. George spoke to her, telling her that the Señorita had been made very happy by Maria's gift, she would doubtless be going up to the village later on in the day, in order to thank Maria personally. Juanita beamed more widely than ever, and tossed her head, and carried the tray back to the kitchen. Selina picked up an *ensamada* and said, "What are these?"

He told her. "They are made each morning by the baker in San Estaban, and Juanita buys them for me and brings them, fresh, for my breakfast."

"Ensamadas." She took a mouthful off the end of one, and soft, flaky bread and sugar encrusted her mouth. "Does Juanita work for anybody else, or just for you?"

"She works for her husband and her children. In the fields and in the house. She has never done anything but work, all her life. Work and get married and go to church and have babies."

"She seems so content, doesn't she? Always smiling."

"She has the shortest legs in the world. Have you noticed?"

"But having short legs has nothing to do with being content."

"No, but it makes her one of the few women in the world who can scrub a floor without kneeling down."

When breakfast was over and before it got too warm, they walked up to the village to do the marketing. Selina wore George's shrunken navy-blue trousers and the espadrilles she had bought in Maria's the day before, and George carried the baskets, and as they walked he taught her to say *"Muchas gracias para las naranjas."*

They went into Maria's shop, through the front section, where the straw hats were piled, and the sun oil and the camera films and the bathing-towels, and into the high, dark room

123

at the back. Here, in the cool, were barrels of wine and bins of sweet-smelling fruit and vegetables, and loaves of bread as long as your arm. Maria, and her husband Pepe, and Tomeu, were all busy serving, and there was a small gathering of waiting customers; but when George and Selina came in, they all stopped talking and looked around, and George gave Selina a prompting dig, and she said, "Maria, *muchas gracias para las naranjas,*" and there was much gap-toothed laughter, and back-slapping as though she had done something enormously clever.

Their baskets were filled with groceries and wine-bottles and bread and fruit, and left for Tomeu to deliver at the Casa Barco on his bicycle. George accepted the glass of brandy offered him by Pepe, and then he and Selina walked over to the Cala Fuerte Hotel to see Rudolfo. They sat at the bar and Rudolfo gave them coffee, and was told that a cable had been sent to England for the money and that very soon, in days, they would be able to repay him, but Rudolfo only laughed and said he did not care how long he had to wait, and George had another brandy and then they said good-bye and walked home again.

Back at the Casa Barco, George dug out the Spanish grammar which had eased him through the intricacies of learning a new language, and gave it to Selina.

She said, "I'm going to start right away."

"Well, before you do, I'm going out to *Eclipse.* Do you want to come too?"

"Are you going to take her for a sail?"

"Take her for a sail? This isn't Frinton, you know." He put on a comic Cockney voice. "Once round the island, arf a crown."

"I just thought you might be going out in her," said Selina, mildly.

"Well, I'm not." He relented. "But I have to take that new propeller out some time, and it might as well be to-day. You could swim if you wanted, but I warn you the water'll be frigid."

"Can I bring the grammar book with me?"

"Bring anything you like. We could take a picnic."

"A picnic!"

"Juanita'll put some food in a basket, I'm sure. It wouldn't exactly be a Fortnum and Mason hamper . . ."

"Oh, do ask her. Then we wouldn't have to come back for lunch."

Half an hour later they piled into the dinghy. Selina sat in the stern, with the box containing the propeller between her knees. She had the grammar book, and a dictionary, and a towel in case she wanted to bathe. The picnic basket lay in the bottom of the boat at George's feet, and George rowed. As they moved away from the slipway, Juanita hung over the terrace and waved a duster, as though she were saying good-bye for ever, and Pearl walked backwards and forwards along the edge of the water mewing plaintively because she had wanted to come too.

"Why can't we take her?" Selina wanted to know.

"She'd hate it once she got there. Too much water gives her traumas."

Selina trailed her hand and gazed down at the depths of waving green weed. "It's like grass, isn't it? Or a forest in the wind." The water was very cold. She withdrew her hand, and turned back to look at the Casa Barco, fascinated by this novel view of it. "It's quite a different shape from all the other houses."

"It was a boat-house. *Barco* is boat."

"Was it a boat-house when you came to live here?"

George rested on his oars. "For the Organising Secretary of the George Dyer Fan Club, you seem to have read my book with remarkably little attention. Or did you read it at all?"

"Yes, I did read it, but I was only looking for things about *you*, because I thought you might be my father. And, of course, there was really nothing about you. It was all about the village and the harbour and *Eclipse* and everything."

George began to row again. "The first time I ever saw Cala Fuerte was from the sea. I'd come from Marseilles, single-handed, because I couldn't pick up a crew, and I had the devil's own job finding the place. I brought *Eclipse* in under power, and I anchored, not a few feet from where she's lying now."

"Did you think then that you'd stay here, and live here, and make it your home?"

"I don't know what I thought. I was too tired to think. But I remember how good the pines smelt in the early morning."

They moved in under *Eclipse'* s hull, and George stood up and took hold of the guard-rail and, holding the painter, climbed up on to the stern deck and made the dinghy fast, and then returned to help Selina unload. She handed up her towel and her book and the picnic basket and then scrambled up herself while George returned to the dinghy to deal with the heavy box containing the propeller.

The tarpaulin cockpit cover was still draped over the coach roof as George had left it, and bone-dry again after its soaking. Selina stepped down into the cockpit and put the picnic basket down on to one of the seats, and looked about her with the confused admiration of one who has never been in a small boat in her life.

She said, "She seems terribly small."

"What did you expect? The *Queen Mary*?" George dumped the propeller onto the floor of the cockpit, and squatted to shove it, out of harm's way, under one of the slatted seats.

"No, of course not."

He stood up. "Come along; I'll show you around."

The steps of the main hatch led down into the galley, a portion of which had been fitted out as a navigation table, with drawers beneath wide enough for charts. Beyond this was the cabin, with two berths on either side of a folding table. Selina asked if this was where George slept, and when George said it was, she pointed out that while he was a good six feet, the bunks could only be four and a half feet long. George, with the air of a conjurer, showed her how the ends of the bunks extended beneath the sideboards.

"Oh, I see. So you sleep with your feet in a hole."

"That's the idea. And very cosy it is, too."

There were a great many books, held in position on their shelves by retainer bars, and the cushions on the berths were blue and red, and a paraffin lamp swung on gimbals. There were some photographs of *Eclipse* under sail, complete with the ballooning stripes of a massive spinnaker, and a locker door, left open, bulged with yellow oilskins. George went forward, easing his way around the white painted column of the mast, and Selina followed him and in the tiny triangular forepeak there was a lavatory, and the chain and sail lockers.

She said again, "It seems so small. I can't imagine living in such close quarters."

"You get used to it. And when you're single-handed, you live in the cockpit. That's why the galley's so handy, so that you can reach in and grab sustenance when you're under way. Come on, let's go back."

Selina went ahead, and behind her he paused to unscrew the portholes and push them open. In the galley, she reached through the hatch for the picnic basket and brought it in, out of the sun. There was a slim-necked bottle of wine which felt sadly warm, but when she told George about this, he produced a length of twine and tied it around the neck of the bottle and hung it overboard. Then he went below again and returned, carrying one of the foam-rubber mattresses from the cabin berth.

"What's that for?"

"I thought you'd like to sunbathe." He heaved it up on to the coach roof.

"What are you going to do? Are you going to fit the propeller?"

"No, I'll wait till the sea warms up a bit, or get someone else to do it for me." He disappeared below again, and Selina took the Spanish grammar and climbed up on to the coach roof and draped herself over the mattress. She opened the grammar and read, "Nouns are either masculine or feminine. They should always be learned with the definite article."

It was very warm. She dropped her head on the open book and closed her eyes. There was the lap of water and the smell of pines and comforting heat of the sun. She spread her arms to its warmth, and her hands and her fingers, and the rest of the world slid away, so that reality was here and now, a white yacht anchored in a blue inlet, with George Dyer moving about below, in the cabin, opening and shutting lockers and occasionally swearing when he dropped something.

Later, she opened her eyes, and said, "George."

"Umm. . . ?" He was sitting in the cockpit naked to the waist, smoking a cigarette, and winding a rope into an immaculate coil.

"I know about masculine and feminine now."

"Well, that's a good start."

"I thought I might swim."

"Well, swim then."

She sat up, pushing her hair back from her face.

"Will it be terribly cold?"

"After Frinton, nothing could be cold."

"How did you know I used to go to Frinton?"

"It's a primeval instinct I have about you. I see you spending your summers there with Nanny. Blue with cold, and shivering."

"You're right, of course. And there are pebbles on the beach, and I always had an enormous sweater over my bathing-suit. Agnes used to hate it, too. Goodness knows why we got sent there."

She stood up and began to unbutton her shirt.

George said, "It's very deep. You can swim?"

"Of course I can swim."

"I'll keep the harpoon handy in case of man-eating sharks."

"Oh, funny!" She pulled off the shirt, and she was wearing the bikini he had given her. He said, "Good God!" because it had been meant as a joke, and he had never imagined that she would have the nerve to put it on, but now he felt as if the joke had back-fired and he was left standing with egg all over his face. Again the word innocence stood up and hit him, and he thought, unfairly, of Frances, with her weather-beaten, black-tanned body and the raffish bikinis which on her could never be anything but vulgar.

He was never sure whether Selina heard his astounded exclamation, for at that moment she dived, and he watched her swimming, neatly and without a splash, and with her long hair fanning out in the water behind her like a new and beautiful species of seaweed.

When at last she came in, shuddering with cold, he shoved a towel at her, and went down to the galley to find something for her to eat; a round of bread with some of Juanita's goat's milk cheese. When he returned, she was back on the coach roof, in the sun, rubbing her hair with the towel. She reminded him of Pearl. He gave her the bread and she said, "At Frinton it was always a ginger snap. Agnes used to call them shivery bites."

"She would."

"You mustn't say things like that. You've never even met her."

"I'm sorry."

"You'd probably like her. You'd probably find a lot in common. Agnes always looks desperately cross, but it doesn't mean a thing. Her bark is much worse than her bite."

"Thank you very much."

"It's meant as a compliment. I'm very fond of Agnes."

"Perhaps if I learn to knit you'll grow fond of me too."

"Is there any more bread? I'm still hungry."

He went below again, and when he returned she was lying on her stomach once more, with the grammar book open. She said, "*Yo*—I. *Tú*—you, (familiar), *Usted*—you (polite)."

"Not *Usted*. *Usteth*. . . ." He gave it the subtle Spanish lisp.

"*Usteth* . . ." She took the bread and began to eat it, absently. "You know, it's funny, but although you know quite a lot about me . . . I've had to tell you, of course, because of thinking you were my father . . . but I don't really know anything at all about you."

He did not reply, and she turned to look at him. He was standing in the cockpit, his head on a level with hers and not two feet away, but his face was turned from her; he was watching one of the fishing-boats move out of the harbour across the pellucid, blue-green water, and all she could see was the brown line of forehead and cheek and jaw. He did not even turn when she spoke, but after a little, he said, "No, I don't suppose you do."

"And I was right, wasn't I? *Fiesta at Cala Fuerte* wasn't about you. You hardly came into the book."

The fishing-boat edged between the bearings of the deep-water channel, and George said, "What are you so anxious to know?"

"Nothing." She was wishing already that she had not broached the subject. "Nothing in particular." She turned down the corner of the page of his grammar, and then smoothed it out again quickly because she had been taught that this was a bad habit. "I suppose I'm just being inquisitive. Rodney, my lawyer—you know, I told you—it was he who gave me your book. And when I told him that I thought you were my father and that I wanted to come and find you, he said that I should let the sleeping tiger lie."

"That sounds a very imaginative thing for Rodney to have said." The fishing-boat passed them, moved into deep water, quickened her engines and headed for the open sea. George turned to face her. "Was I the tiger?"

"Not really. He just didn't want me to stir up a lot of complications."

"You didn't take his advice."

"No, I know."

"What are you trying to say?"

"Just that I'm naturally nosy, I suppose. I'm sorry."

"I haven't anything to hide."

"I like to know about people. Their family and their parents."

"My father was killed in nineteen forty."

"*Your* father was killed, too?"

"His destroyer was torpedoed by a U-boat in the Atlantic."

"Was he in the navy?" George nodded. "How old were you?"

"Twelve."

"Did you have brothers and sisters?"

"No."

"What happened to you then?"

"Well, let's see . . . I stayed at school, and then I did my National Service, and then I decided to stay on in the army and take a commission, which I did."

"Didn't you want to be in the navy like your father?"

"No. I thought the army might be more fun."

"And was it?"

"Some of it. Not all of it. And then . . . my Uncle George suggested that as he had no sons of his own, it might be a good idea if I went into the family business."

"What was that?"

"Woollen mills in the West Riding of Yorkshire."

"And you went?"

131

"Yes. It rather seemed to be my duty."

"But you didn't want to."

"No, I didn't want to."

"What happened then?"

He looked vague. "Well, nothing. I stayed in Bradderford for five years, which I'd agreed to do, and then I sold up my share of the business and got out."

"Didn't your Uncle George mind?"

"He wasn't awfully pleased."

"And what did you do then?"

"I bought *Eclipse* on the proceeds and after a few years of wandering I fetched up here and lived happily ever after."

"And then you wrote your book."

"Yes, of course, I wrote my book."

"And that's the most important thing of all."

"Why so important?"

"Because it's creative. It comes from inside you. To be able to write is a gift. I can't do a single thing."

"I can't do a single thing either," said George, "which is why Mr. Rutland sent me that cryptic message through the medium of you."

"Aren't you going to write another book?"

"Believe me, I would if I could. I did start off, but the thing was such a grinding failure I tore it up into little pieces and had a sort of ritual bonfire. It was discouraging, to say the least of it. And I promised the old boy I'd produce a second effort, even if it was only an idea, within a year, but of course I haven't. I've been told I'm suffering from a writer's block, which, if you're interested, is like the worst sort of mental constipation."

"What did you try to write the second book about?"

"A voyage I did to the Aegean, before I came to live here."

"What went wrong?"

"It was tedious. It was a super trip, but the way I wrote

132

about it, it sounded about as exciting as a bus ride through Leeds on a wet Sunday in November. Anyway, it's all been done before."

"But that isn't the point. Surely you have to find an original angle, or a new approach. Isn't that how it works?"

"Well, of course." He smiled at her. "You're not as green as you're cabbage-looking."

"You say nice things in a horrible way."

"I know. I'm twisted and warped. Now, how about those personal pronouns?"

Selina looked back at the book. "*Usted.* You. *El.* He. *Ella. . . .*"

"You pronounce a double 'l' as though it had a 'y' behind it. *Elya.*"

"*Elya,*" said Selina, and looked up at him again. "Were you never married?"

He did not reply at once, but his face tensed up as though she had switched on a light and held it to his eyes. Then he said, calmly enough, "I never married. But I was once engaged." Selina waited, and, perhaps encouraged by her silence, he went on. "It was while I was in Bradderford. Her parents were Bradderford people, very rich, very kind, self-made. The salt of the earth, really. The father drove a Bentley and the mother drove a Jaguar, and Jenny had a hunter about ten feet high, and a patent automatic horse-box, and they used to go to San Moritz to ski, and to Formentor for their summer holidays, and to the Leeds Music Festival, because they thought it was expected of them."

"I don't know whether you're being kind or cruel."

"I don't know either."

"But why did she break it off?"

"She didn't. I did. Two weeks before the biggest wedding Bradderford had ever known. For months I couldn't get near Jenny for bridesmaids and trousseaux and caterers and photographers and wedding-presents. Oh, God, those wedding-presents! And it began to be like a high wall between us, so that I couldn't get near her. And when I realised that she didn't mind about the wall, she didn't even know it was there . . . well, I've never had an awful lot of self-respect, but what I did have I wanted to keep."

"Did you tell her you weren't going to marry her?"

"Yes. I went to her house. I told Jenny and then I told her parents. And it all took place in a room filled with crates and boxes and tissue paper and silver candlesticks and salad bowls and tea-sets and hundreds of toast racks. It was gruesome. Ghastly." He shuddered slightly at the memory. "I felt like a murderer."

Selina thought of the new flat, of the carpets and the chintzes, the ritual of the white dress and the church wedding and having Mr. Arthurstone to give her away. The panic that suddenly visited her was the panic of a bad dream. Of being lost, and knowing that you were lost. Knowing that somewhere you had taken the wrong turning and ahead there could be nothing but disaster, precipitous cliffs and every sort of nameless fear. She wanted to leap to her feet, to escape and run away from everything she had ever committed herself to doing.

"Was . . . was that when you left Bradderford?"

"Don't look so horrified. No, it wasn't; I had another two years to run. I spent them being *persona non grata* with all the debs' mums and being cut by all sorts of unexpected people. It was rather interesting in a way, finding out who my real friends were . . ." He moved forward to rest his elbows on the edge of the coach roof. "But all this is doing nothing to improve your faultless Castilian Spanish. See if you can say the present tense of *Hablar.*"

Selina started. "*Hablo.* I speak. *Usted habla,* you speak. Were you in love with her?"

George glanced up swiftly, but there was no anger in his dark eyes, only pain. Then he put his brown hand flat over the open page of the Spanish grammar and said gently, "Without looking. You mustn't cheat."

The Citröen nosed into Cala Fuerte at the very hottest time of the day. The sun shimmered in a sky of cloudless blue, shadows were black, and dust and houses very white. There was no living soul about; shutters were closed, and as Frances drew up in front of the Cala Fuerte Hotel, and turned off the engine of the powerful car, there was a great silence, broken only by the rustle of the pines which moved in some mysterious, unfelt breeze.

She got out of the car, and slammed the door shut, and went up the steps of the hotel and in through the chain curtain to Rudolfo's bar. After the sunshine it took a moment for her eyes to become accustomed to the darkness, but Rudolfo was there, stealing a siesta in one of the long cane chairs, and he woke as she came in, and stood up, sleepy and surprised.

She said, "Well, hello, *amigo.*"

He rubbed his eyes. "Francesca! What are you doing here?"

"Just drove over from San Antonio. Could you give me a drink?"

He moved behind his bar. "What do you want?"

"Any cold beer?" She pulled herself up on to a stool, and took out a cigarette, and lit it from the box of matches that Rudolfo pushed across to her. He opened the beer and poured it, carefully, without a head. He said, "It's not a good time of the day to be driving an open car."

"Doesn't bother me."

"It is very hot for so early in the year."

"This is the hottest day we've had yet. San Antonio is like a tin of sardines; it's a relief to get out into the country."

"Is that why you're here?"

"Not entirely. I came to see George."

Rudolfo replied to this in a characteristic way which was

135

to shrug and turn down the corners of his mouth. It seemed to suggest some innuendo, and Frances frowned. "Isn't he here?"

"But of course he is here." A gleam of malice showed in Rudolfo's eyes. "Did you know that he had a visitor staying at the Casa Barco?"

"A visitor?"

"His daughter."

"*Daughter!*" After a second's astounded silence, Frances laughed. "Are you crazy?"

"I am not crazy. His daughter is here."

"But . . . but George has never been married."

"I don't know about that," said Rudolfo.

"How old is she, for heaven's sake?"

He shrugged again. "Seventeen?"

"But it's impossible . . ."

Rudolfo began to be annoyed. "Francesca, I tell you she is there."

"I saw George in San Antonio yesterday. Why didn't he say anything?"

"Did he give you no idea?"

"No. No, he didn't."

But this was not strictly true, because all his actions yesterday had been unusual and therefore, in Frances's eyes, faintly suspect. The sudden urge to send a cable when he had been in the town only the previous day, the purchase made in Teresa's, that most feminine of shops, and his final remarks about having more to feed than the cat when he returned to Cala Fuerte. All evening and most of the night, she had been chewing over these three clues, convinced that they all added up to something about which she ought to know, and this morning, unable to remain in ignorance any longer, she had decided to come to Cala Fuerte and find out what was going on. Even if there was nothing to discover, she would see George. And it was true that the congested streets and pavements of San Antonio had begun to get on her nerves, and the thought of the empty blue inlets and the fresh piny smell of Cala Fuerte was very inviting.

And now this. It was his daughter. George had a daughter. She stubbed out her cigarette, and saw that her hand was shaking. She said, as calmly and as casually as she could, "What is she called?"

"The señorita? Selina."

"Selina." She said the name as though it left a bad taste in her mouth.

"She is very charming."

Frances finished her beer. She set down the empty glass, and said, "I think I'd better go and find out for myself."

"You should do that."

She slid off the high stool and picked up her bag and made for the door. But at the chain curtain, she stopped and turned, and Rudolfo was watching her with a gleam of amusement in his frog-eyes.

"Rudolfo, if I wanted to stay for the night . . . would you have a room for me?"

"Of course, Francesca. I will have one made ready."

She drove, in a cloud of dust, to the Casa Barco, left the Citröen in the only patch of shade she could find, and crossed the lane to the house. She opened the green shutter door, and called, "Anyone around?" but there was no reply, so she went in.

The place was empty. It smelt sweetly, of wood ash and fruit, and was cool with the air that moved in from the sea through the open windows. She dropped her bag on a handy chair, and wandered round, searching for signs of feminine occupation, but there appeared to be none. From the gallery there was a small sound, but when she looked up, a little startled, it was only George's ridiculous white cat jumping off the bed, and coming down the steps to welcome the visitor. Frances did not like cats, especially this one, and gave Pearl a push with her foot, but Pearl's dignity was not impaired. Her back view speaking volumes, she left Frances and walked, tail erect, out on to the terrace. After a moment Frances followed her, lifting George's binoculars off his table as she went by. *Eclipse* lay quietly at anchor. Frances raised the binoculars and focused them and the yacht and her occupants sprang towards her. George was in the cockpit, at full length on one of the seats, his old cap tipped over his eyes, and a book on his chest. The girl was draped over the coach roof, an arrangement of boneless-looking limbs and a quantity of pale fawn hair. She wore a shirt which looked as though it might belong to George, and Frances could not see her face. The little scene was one of content and companionship, and Frances was frowning when she lowered the binoculars. She returned them to the table, and then went to draw herself a glass of George's sweet, cool well water. She brought the glass back on to the terrace, pulled the least lethal of his terrace chairs back into the shade of the split-cane awning, stretched herself gingerly out, and settled down to wait.

George said, "Are you awake?"

"Yes."

"I think we should get straightened up and go back. You've been out in the sun for long enough."

Selina sat up and stretched. "I went to sleep."

"I know."

"It was all that gorgeous wine."

"Yes, I expect it was."

They rowed back to the Casa Barco, the dinghy suspended like a cloud over the peacock-coloured water, her shadow drifting through the weeds below them. The world was still and hot and quiet, and seemed to contain only the two of them. Selina's skin prickled and felt tight, as though, like an over-ripe fruit, she might burst out of it, but this sensation was not unpleasant—merely a part of the splendid day. She pulled the empty basket between her knees and said, "That was a good picnic. The best I ever had," and waited for George to come back with some crack about Frinton, but to her surprised delight he said nothing, only smiled at her as though he had enjoyed it too.

He brought the dinghy up to the jetty and stepped ashore and made her fast with two loops of the painter. Selina handed out all their gear, and then stepped after him, the jetty burning hot on the soles of her bare feet, and they crossed the slipways, and started up the steps to the terrace, George going ahead, so that Selina, behind him, heard Frances Dongen's voice before she ever saw her.

"Well, now. Look who's here!"

For a split second George appeared to be petrified into stillness. And then, as though nothing had ever been said, he went on, up to the terrace.

"Hello, Frances," he said.

Selina, more slowly, followed him. Frances lay in the old cane chair, with her feet up on the table. She wore a blue-and-white-checked shirt, knotted to expose her dark-tanned midriff, and white duck pants, skimpy and tight. She had kicked off her shoes, and her feet, crossed on the edge of the table, were dark and dusty, the toe-nails lacquered bright red. She made no effort to sit up or get up, but merely lay there, supine, her hands resting on the floor, and surveyed George from under her thatch of short blonde hair.

"Isn't this a nice surprise?" She looked over his shoulder and saw Selina. "Hi, there!"

Selina smiled weakly. "Hello."

George put down the basket. "What are you doing here?"

"Well, San Antonio's pretty hot and full and noisy, and I thought I might give myself a couple of days off."

"Are you staying here?"

"Rudolfo said he'd give me a room."

"You've seen Rudolfo?"

139

"Yeah, I had a drink with him on my way here." She eyed him, her eyes malicious, teasing him because he didn't know how much Rudolfo had told her.

George sat on the edge of the table. "Did Rudolfo tell you I had Selina staying with me?"

"Oh, sure, he told me." She smiled at Selina. "You know, you're the biggest surprise that ever happened to me. George, you haven't introduced us yet."

"Sorry. Selina, this is Mrs. Dongen . . ."

"Frances," said Frances quickly.

"And this is Selina Bruce."

Selina moved forward with her hand outstretched to say "How do you do," but Frances ignored the tentative gesture.

"Are you here on a visit?"

"Yes, I am. . . ."

"George, you never told me you had a daughter."

George said, "She isn't my daughter."

Frances, blank-faced, seemed to accept this. Then she lifted her foot from the table's edge and pulled herself into a sitting position. "Are you trying to tell me . . ."

"Hang on a moment. Selina . . ."

She turned to look at him, and he saw that she was confused and embarrassed, and even, possibly, a little hurt. He said, "Would you mind if I spoke to Frances alone, just for a moment?"

"No. No, of course not." She tried to smile, to show how little she minded, and swiftly laid down the things she had been carrying, the towel and the Spanish grammar, as though to lighten herself before making a swift escape.

"Just for five minutes . . ."

"I'll go back down to the dinghy. It's cool there."

"Yes, do that."

She went, swiftly, away and out of sight down the steps. In a moment Pearl, who had been sitting on the terrace wall, stood up and stretched, leapt lightly down, and went off after her. George turned back to Frances. He said again, "She isn't my daughter."

"Well, who the hell is she?"

"She arrived here from London, out of the blue, looking for me, because she thought I was her father."

"What made her think that?"

"The photograph on the back of my book."

"Do you *look* like her father?"

"Yes, I do. In fact, he was a distant cousin of mine, but that's beside the point. He's dead. He's been dead for years. He was killed in the war."

"She surely didn't imagine he'd come alive again?"

"I suppose if you want something badly enough you can believe in any miracle."

"Rudolfo told me that she *was* your daughter."

"Yes, I know. The buzz got round the village, and for her sake it seemed kinder not to deny it. She'd already been here for two days."

"Living here—with you? You must be out of your mind."

"She had to stay. The airline had lost her luggage, and her return ticket was stolen at the airport."

"Why didn't you tell me about her yesterday?"

"Because it didn't seem to be any of your business." This sounded ruder than he had intended. "Oh, God, I'm sorry, but it's just the way things are."

"What are your friends in Cala Fuerte going to say when they know she isn't your daughter? When they know you've been lying to them. . . ."

"I'll explain when she's gone."

"And when might that be?"

"When we get some cash from London. We already owe Rudolfo six hundred pesetas, and we have to buy another air ticket, and my own money's been held up in Barcelona . . ."

"You mean it's only money!" George stared at her. "That's

141

the only thing that's kept her here? That's the only reason you didn't send her straight back home?"

"It's as good a reason as any."

"But, for Pete's sake, why didn't you come to me?"

George opened his mouth to tell her why and then shut it again. Frances was incredulous. "Does she want to stay here? Do you *want* her here?"

"No, of course not. She can't wait to get back, and I can't wait to be rid of her. But meantime, the situation's quite harmless."

"Harmless? That's the most naïve thing I've ever heard you say. Why, this situation is about as harmless as a barrel of dynamite."

He did not reply, but sat, shoulders hunched, his hands closed so tightly over the edge of the table that the knuckles shone white. Frances, with a show of gentle understanding, laid her hand over his, and he did not try to move away. She said, "You've confided in me now, so let me help. There's a seven o'clock plane this evening from San Antonio to Barcelona. There's a connection to London, and she should be back by midnight. I'll give her enough for the journey, and to get her back to where she lives." He still said nothing, and she went on, gently, "Darling, this isn't any time to dither. I'm right, and you know it. She can't stay here any longer."

Selina was sitting on the end of the jetty, with her back to the house, trailing her feet in the water. He came down the steps from the terrace and across the slipways and down the sagging planking, his footsteps echoing, but she did not turn around. He said her name, but she would not answer. He squatted to her height.

"Listen. I want to talk to you."

She leaned away from him, out over the water, and her hair parted on the nape of her neck and fell down on either side of her face.

"Selina, try to understand."

"You haven't said anything yet."

"You can go back to London, to-night. There's a plane at seven; you should be home by midnight, or one in the morning at the latest. Frances says she'll pay for your ticket. . . ."

"Do you want me to go?"

"It's not a case of what I want, or what you want. We have to do what is right and what is going to be best for you. I suppose I should never have let you stay here in the first place, but circumstances did rather run away with us. Let's face it; Cala Fuerte isn't exactly the place for someone like you, and poor Agnes is bound to be anxious about what's happening. I really think that you should go."

Selina took her long legs out of the water, and pulled her knees up to her chin, hugging them as though she were trying to hold herself together, to stop herself from falling apart.

He said, "I'm not sending you away . . . it has to be your own decision. . . ."

"It's very kind of your friend."

"She wants to help."

"If I'm going to go back to London to-night," said Selina, "I haven't very much time."

"I'll drive you to San Antonio."

"No!" She startled him with her vehemence, turning to look at him for the first time. "No, I don't want you to come. Surely someone else can take me! Rudolfo, or a taxi or something. There must be someone."

He tried not to show his hurt. "Well, of course, but . . ."

"I don't want you to take me."

"All right. It doesn't matter."

"And in London I'll call Agnes from the airport. She'll be home; I can get a taxi, and she'll be waiting for me."

It was as though she had already gone, and they were both alone. She was alone in the plane, alone in London, cold, because after San Antonio it would be very cold; trying to ring

143

Agnes from a call box. And it would be past midnight and Agnes would be asleep and would wake slowly. The telephone would ring in the empty flat, and Agnes would get up and pull on her dressing-gown and go, switching on lights as she went, to answer the call. And after that to fill a hot water bottle, to turn down a bed, put milk on to heat.

But beyond, he could not see.

He said, "What will you do? When you get back to London? I mean, when all this is over and forgotten?"

"I don't know."

"Hadn't you any plans?"

After a little, she shook her head.

"Make some," he said, gently. "Good ones."

10

_**~~~**_

It was decided that Pepe, the husband of Maria, should be approached and asked if he would take Selina to the airport. Pepe did not run an official taxi service, but on occasion he would clean his aged car of the old straw and hen manure and such agricultural flotsam as it was normally encrusted with, and convey stray travellers to wherever they wanted to go. George, driving Frances's car, went to seek Pepe out, and ask if he would do this thing, and Selina, left alone with Frances and Pearl at the Casa Barco, prepared for her departure.

It did not take very long. She took a shower and dressed, in George's trousers that Juanita had so lovingly shrunk, and the striped shirt, and the espadrilles that she had bought in Maria's shop. Her good jersey dress had already been bequeathed to Juanita as a duster, and her bikini was so small that it fitted without fuss into the bottom of her handbag. That

145

was all. She combed her hair and put her coat over a handy chair, and reluctantly, because she did not want to talk, went out on to the terrace, where Frances had collapsed once more into the long chair. Her eyes were closed, but when she heard Selina approach, she opened them and turned her head to watch Selina as she came to sit on the terrace wall, facing her.

"All packed?" she asked.

"Yes."

"That didn't take long."

"I didn't have any clothes. I lost my case. It got sent to Madrid by mistake."

"Those sort of mistakes are always happening." She sat up and reached for her packet of cigarettes. "Smoke?"

"No, thank you."

Frances lit one for herself. "I hope you don't think I'm interfering, chasing you out of the place like this."

"No. I had to get back anyway. The sooner I get home the better."

"Do you live in London?"

"Yes." She made herself say it. "Queen's Gate."

"How nice. Have you enjoyed your visit to San Antonio?"

Selina said, "It's been very interesting."

"You thought George was your father."

"I thought he might have been. But I was wrong."

"Did you read his book?"

"I haven't read it properly yet. But I will when I get home. I'll have time then." She added, "It's been a great success."

"Oh, sure," said Frances, dismissing the book.

"Didn't you think it was good?"

"Yes, it was good. It was fresh and original." She took a long pull on her cigarette, dropped the ash on to the floor of the terrace. "But he won't write another."

Selina frowned. "What makes you say that?"

146

"Because I don't think he has the self-discipline to get down to a second book."

"He's been told he's suffering from writer's block."

Frances laughed. "Look, darling, it was I who told him that."

"If you don't think he is capable of writing a second book, why did you say he was suffering from writer's block?"

"Oh, because he was depressed, and I was trying to cheer him up. George doesn't need to write. He has money of his own, and the sheer hard labour of writing simply isn't worth the candle."

"But he *must* write another book."

"Why?"

"Because he agreed to. Because the publisher is waiting for it. For his own sake."

"That's just a lot of hooey."

"Don't you *want* him to go on writing?"

"What I want or what I don't want is immaterial. I am merely stating an opinion. Look, honey, I run an art gallery. I deal all the time with these temperaments, these artists, these moods. I just don't think George is a creative artist."

"But if he doesn't write, what will he do?"

"What he did before he wrote *Fiesta at Cala Fuerte.* Nothing. It's easy to do nothing in San Antonio, to say '*Mañana*' to everything." She smiled. "Don't look so shocked. George and I are twice your age, and at forty some of your illusions and your bright dreams get a bit bumped at the corners. Life doesn't have to be so real and so earnest as it does at eighteen . . . or whatever you are. . . ."

"I'm twenty," said Selina. Her voice was suddenly cold and Frances was pleased, because she thought she had annoyed her. She lay, watching Selina, and she was not afraid anymore, as she had been when she first saw her, because Selina was going; in half an hour she would be on her way. To

147

the airport, to London, back to a life in Queen's Gate about which Frances was content to remain in total ignorance.

The sound of the returning Citröen disturbed their uneasy silence, followed by the less sophisticated grinding of Pepe's ancient car. Selina stood up. "There's the taxi, now."

"Oh, fine!" Frances stubbed her cigarette out on to the floor. "Here, I'll give you the money."

She could scarcely bear to take it, but it was being counted into her palm when George came through the house to join them. He looked as uncomfortable as Selina about the whole business, but only pointed out that Selina would need sterling in London, whereupon Frances signed one of her American Express cheques and handed that over too.

"You can get it cashed at the airport."

"It's very kind of you."

"Oh, it's a pleasure," said Frances. "Think nothing of it."

"I . . . I'll make certain you're paid back. . . ."

"Yes, of course you will."

George said, "Where's your bag?"

"Inside."

He went to get it, and it was he who took the money from Selina and stowed it away in a secure and well-hidden inner pocket. "Don't lose it again," he said; "I couldn't stand the strain." It had been meant as a feeble joke, but was instantly regretted because it sounded as though he couldn't bear the thought of once more being landed with her. He said, quickly, to cover up, "You've got your passport?" She nodded. "You're sure?"

"Yes, of course."

"I think perhaps you should make a start. There's not all that much time to spare. . . ."

She was being eased, gently, but firmly, away. She would never come back. Slowly, she followed George back into the house. He picked up her porridge-coloured coat, and moved aside, as though to let her go ahead of him. Behind her, Frances Dongen stood in the open terrace doorway.

He said quite gently, "Pepe's waiting . . ."

Selina swallowed. She said, "I'm suddenly very thirsty. Have I got time to have a drink . . . ?"

"But of course." He moved towards the well, but Selina said, "No. I'd rather have soda water, it's more refreshing and so cold. Don't bother. I'll get it. There's some in the fridge. I won't be a moment."

They waited while she went for the drink, slipping behind the counter of the galley, and stooping to open the refrigerator and take out a frosty bottle. For a moment she was invisible, and then she stood up, holding the bottle, and opened it, and poured it into a tumbler, and drank it so quickly that George said that she would surely explode.

"I won't explode." She put down the empty glass and suddenly smiled. It was as though the glass of soda water had solved all her problems. "It was delicious."

They went out into the sunshine, and Pepe waited for them. Pepe took Selina's coat and laid it with care over the hastily-cleaned back seat, and Selina said good-bye to Frances, and thanked her for all her help, and then she turned to George. She did not hold out her hand and he could not kiss her. They said good-bye without touching, but he felt as though he were being torn apart.

She got into the old car, erect and touching and hideously vulnerable, and Pepe got in beside her, and George gave him half a dozen last-minute instructions, and threatened death if anything should go wrong, and Pepe understood, and nodded, and even laughed toothlessly as he put the old car into gear.

It ground away up the hill and away from them, and George went on watching, long after it was out of sight, because he could still hear the sound of the engine.

* * *

There was a great party that night in the Cala Fuerte Hotel. It was not planned, but it evolved, in the way that the best parties do, growing and expanding to include a dozen different nationalities and a terrifying amount of drink. Everybody got very gay. A fat girl decided that she would dance on the table, but fell off into the arms of her boyfriend and remained there, asleep, for the rest of the evening. One of the boatmen from the harbour produced his guitar and a Frenchwoman did a mock flamenco which seemed to George the funniest thing he had ever seen in his life. At about one in the morning, however, he suddenly announced that he was going home, back to the Casa Barco. There was a great howl of protestation, taunts of being a kill-joy, claims that it was his turn to stand the drinks, but he remained adamant, because he knew that he must get out before he stopped laughing and started to cry. There was nothing worse than a maudlin drunk.

He stood up, pushing back his chair from the table with a head-splitting sound. Frances said, "I'll come too."

"You're staying here, remember."

"I'll drive you home. What's the good of walking when there's a perfectly good car at the door?"

He gave in, because it was simpler and less effort than having a scene. Outside, the warm southern night was bright with starlight. The Citröen was parked in the middle of the square, and as they walked towards her, Frances slid the car keys into George's hand and said, "You drive."

She was perfectly capable of driving herself, but every now and then liked to pretend that she was helpless and feminine, so George took the keys and got in behind the wheel.

It occurred to him that while his own ridiculous little yellow-wheeled car was merely a method of getting about the island, Frances's Citröen, fast and powerful, was somehow a sexy extension of her own personality. She sat beside him now with her face tipped up to the stars, her brown neck plunged into the deep V of her low-buttoned shirt. He knew that she was waiting to be kissed, but he lit a cigarette, before he started the engine, and she said, "Why don't you kiss me?"

George said, "I mustn't kiss you; I don't know where you've been."

"Why do you have to turn everything into a joke?"

"It's my British defence mechanism."

She glanced at her watch, clear in the starlight. "It's one o'clock. Do you think she'll be back in London?"

"She should be."

"Queen's Gate. Not really our line of country, darling."

He began to whistle, beneath his breath, a tune that had been plaguing him, at the back of his brain, all evening. "You aren't worrying about her, are you?"

"No, I'm not worrying. I should have taken her to the airport though, not let her go with Pepe in that sewing-machine on wheels he calls a car."

"She didn't want you to take her. She would have howled all over you, and you would both have been embarrassed." He made no answer to this, and she laughed. "You're like a stubborn bear that won't bait."

"I'm too drunk to bait."

"Let's go home."

He drove back, still whistling that damned tune. When they got to the Casa Barco and George killed the engine and got out of the car, Frances got out too. As though it had been planned, she came in with him, and the house was cool and dark, but he turned on the lights and went, automatically, to pour himself a drink, because without a drink he would die, or go to sleep and burst into tears, and he was damned if he would do any of these things with Frances watching him.

She flopped, entirely at home, on to his sofa, her feet on one arm, and her curly head propped up by a sky-blue cushion. He fumbled his way through pouring a couple of drinks, dropped the opener and spilt the ice, and Frances said, "That's the hell of a tune you're whistling. Don't you know any other?"

"I don't even know what it is."

"Well, stop anyway."

His head was thumping, there seemed to be pools of water and melting ice everywhere and he couldn't find anything with which to wipe it all up. He picked up the drinks, and took them over to where Frances lay, and she took hers, but all the time her eyes were on his face, and he sat on the hearth with his back to the empty fireplace, and his own drink cradled between his hands.

She said, untroubled, "You know, darling, you're mad at me."

"I am?"

"Sure you are."

"Why?"

"Because I got rid of your little girl-friend. And because you know in your heart of hearts, you should have done that for yourself. And right away."

"I couldn't buy an air ticket without any money."

"That, if you don't mind my saying so, is the feeblest excuse any man gave to himself."

He looked down at his drink. "Yes," he said at last. "Maybe it is."

The tune went on and on in the back of his mind. After a little, Frances said, "When you went off to find Pepe and that child was getting ready to go, I had a little mosey round your desk. You don't seem to be exactly productive."

"I'm not. I haven't written a word."

"Have you replied to dear Mr. Rutland?"

"No. I haven't done that either. But," he added with a touch of malice, "I've consulted a specialist and been told I'm suffering from writer's block."

"Well," said Frances, with some satisfaction, "at least that's a flash of your ornery self. And if you take your kid gloves off, then I can too. You see, darling, I don't think you're ever going to write that second book."

"What makes you so sure?"

"Just you. The way you are. Writing's hard labour, and you're one of those classic, no-good, expatriate Englishmen who do nothing more gracefully than any race alive." He acknowledged this with a spontaneous gleam of amusement, and Frances sat up, encouraged, because she had not lost her gift for making him laugh. "George, if you don't want to go to Malagar, if you don't enjoy the bull-fighting, then I don't want to go either. But why don't we get away together? We could take *Eclipse* to Sardinia, or go overland to Australia, or . . . ride a camel through the Gobi desert . . ."

"Bags on the front hump."

"You're turning everything into a joke again. I'm serious. We're free and we have all the time in the world. Why flog yourself to bits over a typewriter? Is there anything left, in the world, that you can write about really well?"

"Frances, I don't know."

She fell back on to the cushion. She had finished her drink, and dropped the empty glass down on the floor beside her. She was sprawled, seductive, raffish, frighteningly familiar. She said, "I love you. You must know that."

There seemed no reason not to make love to her. He set down his glass, and went to sit beside her, to pull her into his arms, and kiss her as though he wanted to drown himself. She made small, pleasurable noises, and writhed her hands in his hair, and he took his mouth from hers and rubbed his cheek down the sharp angle of her jaw, and could feel the roughness of his beard scraping her skin, and she buried her face in his shoulder and her strong arms were like a vice about his neck.

She said, "Do you love me?" but he could not answer, so she said instead, "Do you like me? Do you want me?"

He took her arms from his neck, and pulled himself free, and was left sitting, holding her forearms as though they had been fighting.

She began to laugh. Her resilience and her good-humour

153

were two of the good things that he had always liked about her. She said, "Why, I believe you're punch drink."

He got up and went to find some cigarettes, and behind him Frances pulled herself off the sofa, and ran her fingers through her hair. She said, "I must patch myself up before I go back to Rudolfo. He's old-fashioned, you know, about so many things. Mind if I used your bedroom?"

"Go ahead," said George, and switched on the upstairs light for her.

She ran up the steps, the heels of her sandals slapping on the wooden treads. She was singing the song that had been tormenting him all evening, and still it did not have any words, and then, as though someone had switched off a radio, the teasing tune was stopped, and Frances was silent. The silence caught at George, as surely as though she had suddenly screamed. He stopped prowling, and pricked up his ears like a suspicious dog.

Presently, Frances came down the steps again, with an expression on her face that he could not begin to decipher. He said stupidly, "What's up? No comb?"

"I don't know," said Frances. "I didn't look. I didn't look farther than the bed . . ."

"The bed?" He was completely mystified.

"It couldn't be a joke? Not another example of that peer-less British sense of humour?"

He realised then, to his horror, that she was really angry. Beneath the careful control of her voice was the tremor of an incipient explosion.

"Frances, I don't know what you're talking about."

"The girl. Your daughter. Selina. Whatever you like to call her. You know where she is? Not in London. Not even at the airport at San Antonio. She's up there . . ." She pointed a shaking finger and her control, like an overstretched rubber band, suddenly cracked. *"In your bed!"*

"I don't believe it."

"Well, go and take a look. *Go on up and take a look.*" He did not move. "I don't know what's going on here, George, but I didn't hand over a considerable amount of pesetas just to find that little tramp back in your bed again . . ."

"She isn't a tramp."

". . . and if you're going to try and give me some sort of an explanation, it had better be good, because I'm not going to swallow a second load of hog wash about losing luggage and thinking you were her long-lost daddy. . . ."

"It was true."

"True? Look, you bastard, who do you think you're kidding?" She was shouting at him now, and it was the one thing that made him mad.

"I didn't know she'd come back . . ."

"Well, kick her out now . . ."

"I'll do no such thing . . ."

"Right." Frances swooped to gather up her handbag. "If you feel inclined to set up house with that mealy-mouthed little tramp, that's O.K. by me . . ."

"Shut up!"

". . . but don't involve me in a complicated scheme to protect both your reputations, because as far as I'm concerned, they're simply not worth protecting." She made for the door and flung it wide, turning back to deliver a final broadside, as she did so, but the effect was slightly spoiled by the entrance of Pearl, erect and dignified. She had been outside the door waiting for someone to let her in, and when Frances did just this thing, entered with a faint mew of appreciation and thanks.

"You'd better go," George said, as calmly as he could, and Frances said, "Don't bother; I've gone!" and pausing only to give Pearl a vicious kick in passing, she was out of the door, and slamming it so hard behind her that the whole house shook.

In a moment the quiet night was torn asunder by the

sound of the Citröen being brutally started and driven up the hill in bottom gear at a speed that set George's teeth on edge.

He stooped to pick up Pearl. Her feelings were hurt, but there was no further damage, and he sat her gently on her favourite cushion on the sofa. A slight movement above him made him look up. Selina was standing, her hands on the rail of the gallery, watching him. She was wearing a white nightgown with blue ribbons framing the neck, and she said, anxiously, "Is Pearl all right?"

"Yes, she's all right. What are you doing here?"

"I was in bed. Asleep."

"You're not asleep now. Get something on and come on down."

A moment later she descended from the gallery, bare-foot, but tying the ribbons of a ridiculous white silk negligee that matched the nightgown.

He frowned and said, "Where did you get those?"

Selina came across the floor towards him. "My suitcase had come. From Madrid." She smiled, as though he should be pleased, and he was forced to resort to sarcasm.

"So you did get as far as the airport?"

"Oh, yes."

"And what happened this time? The flight was cancelled? There wasn't any room on the plane? Pepe had a puncture?"

"No, none of those things." Her eyes were so wide that the blues were entirely ringed with white. "I lost my passport."

"You *what*?" To his annoyance it came out as an incredulous yelp.

"Yes, it was most extraordinary. You know you asked me, before I left, if I had my passport. Well, it was in my bag then, and I don't remember opening it again, but when I got to the airport and I was buying my ticket and everything, I opened my bag. And it had gone."

She looked at him to gauge his reaction to this piece of

information. George's reaction was to lean against the back of his sofa and maintain a monumental calm.

"I see. So what did you do then?"

"Well, I told the Guardia Civil, of course."

"And what did the Guardia Civil have to say?"

"Oh, he was most kind and understanding. And after a little, I thought I'd better just come back here and wait until they found it."

"Who's they?"

"The Guardia Civil."

There was a small silence, while they watched each other. Then George said, "Selina."

"Yes?"

"Do you know what the Guardia Civil do to people who lose their passports? They throw them into jail. They intern them as political prisoners. They let them rot in dungeons until the passports get found again."

"Well, they didn't do that to me."

"You're lying, aren't you? Where did you put that passport of yours?"

"I don't know. I lost it."

"Did you leave it in Pepe's car?"

"I tell you, it's lost."

"Look, Junior, in Spain passports aren't things you play games with."

"I'm not playing games."

"Did you tell Pepe about the passport?"

"I can't speak Spanish, how could I tell him?"

"You just got him to bring you back?"

She looked disconcerted, but only said, bravely, "Yes."

"When did you get here?"

"About eleven."

"Did we wake you up when we got in?" She nodded. "Then you heard most of our conversation?"

"Well, I did try to put my head under the blankets, but

157

Mrs. Dongen has a very carrying voice. I'm sorry she doesn't like me." There was no comment to be made on this, and she went on, in social tones that would have done credit to her grandmother, "Are you going to marry her?"

"Do you know something? You make me ill."

"Is she married?"

"Not anymore."

"What happened to her husband?"

"I don't know . . . how should I know? Maybe he's dead."

"Did she kill him?"

His hands seemed, suddenly, to have taken on an independent personality of their own. They itched with the desire to take Selina and shake her till her teeth rattled, to box her ears, and slap that smug expression off her face. George slid his hands into his pockets, and balled his fists against these purely primitive instincts, but Selina seemed innocent of the turmoil that was going on within him.

"I suppose it was rather annoying for her, finding me here, but she wouldn't stay and listen to any explanations. She just kicked poor Pearl. . . . It would have been much more fair if she'd kicked me." She looked George straight in the eye and he was shattered by her nerve. "She must know you very well. To talk to you like that, I mean. Like the way she did tonight. She wanted you to make love to her."

"You're asking for trouble, Selina."

"And she seems to think that you'll never write another book."

"She may not be wrong at that."

"Aren't you even going to try?"

George said, slowly, "You mind your own bloody business," but even this did not deter her.

"It seems to me that you're afraid of failing before you've even made a start. Mrs. Dongen was right; you've been cast in a classic mould, one of those no-good expatriate Englishmen" (here Selina gave a startling imitation of Frances's drawl) "who do nothing so gracefully. I suppose it would be a pity to spoil the image. And after all, what does it matter? You don't need to write. It isn't your living. And as for Mr. Rutland, what is a broken promise? It doesn't count for anything. You can break your word to him just as easily as you broke it to the girl you were going to marry."

Before he could think, or control himself, George's right hand had escaped from the prison of his pocket and he had slapped her face. The sound of the blow was as loud a crack as the explosion of a bursting paper bag. The ensuing silence was painful to a degree. Selina stared, incredulous but curiously unresentful while George rubbed his stinging palm against his side. He remembered that he had never got those cigarettes. He went to find them now, to take one out and light it, and he was horrified to see how his hands were shaking. When at last he turned around, he realised, to his horror, that she was trying not to cry. The thought of tears, and the subsequent re-criminations and apologies, was almost more than he could bear. Besides, it was too late to start apologising. He said, impatiently, but not unkindly, "Oh, go on, buzz off!" and when she turned and fled, in a flurry of long bare legs and white silk, back up to his bed he called after her, "And don't slam the door," but the joke was a sour one, and fell as flat as it deserved.

II

It was late when he woke. He knew by the angle of the sunshine, by the reflected water-shadows on the ceiling, by the gentle sounds of sweeping which indicated that Juanita was cleaning the terrace. Instinctively tensed against the hangover which he knew was going to hit him, George reached for his watch, and saw that it was half past ten. He had not slept so late for years.

He moved his head carefully from side to side, waiting for the first stab of his well-deserved agony. Nothing happened. Pushing his luck, he tried rolling his eyes and the sensation was in no way painful. He turned aside the red-and-white blanket, and cautiously sat up. It was a miracle. He felt quite normal; better than normal, bright and alert and full of energy.

Gathering up his clothes, he went to shower and shave. As he scraped away at his face, the tune of last night came back to him, but this time it had words, and he realised, too late by now, why Frances had been so annoyed with him for whistling it.

I've grown accustomed to her face.
She almost makes the day begin.

Well, he asked his sheepish reflection, *and how corny can you get?* But when he had dressed, he went and dug out his old record-player, and rubbed the dust from the Frank Sinatra disc, and put it on.

Juanita had finished scrubbing the terrace, and now, hearing the music, she laid down her brushes and came in, her wet brown feet leaving marks on the tiled floor.

"Señor," she said.

"Juanita! *Buenos días.*"

"The Señor has slept well?"

"Too well, perhaps."

I've grown accustomed to the tune
She whistles night and noon.

"Where is the Señorita?"

"She has gone out to the Señor's boat, to swim."

"How did she get there?"

"She has taken the little boat."

He raised his brows in mild surprise. "Well, good for her. Juanita, is there any coffee?"

"I will make some."

She went to draw a bucket of water, and George realised that he felt well enough to want a cigarette. He found one, and lit it, and then said, cautiously, "Juanita?"

"*Sé,* señor."

"An Americana stayed at the Cala Fuerte Hotel last night . . ."

161

"No, señor."

He frowned. "What do you mean?"

Juanita was in the kitchen, putting on a kettle. "She did not stay, Señor. She drove back to San Antonio last night. She did not use the room at the hotel. Rosita told Tomeu and Tomeu told Maria, and . . ."

"I know; Maria told you." But Juanita's news filled him with a shameful sort of relief, although the thought of Frances hurtling back to San Antonio through the night in that lethal bomb of a car, gave him the shivers. He prayed that nothing had happened, that she had not had an accident, was not, even now, trapped in some distant ditch with the car on top of her.

With the air of a man cornered on all sides by trouble, he scratched the back of his neck, then went out on to the terrace to search for his other headache. He took his binoculars and focused them on *Eclipse*, but although the dinghy bobbed peacefully at her stern, there was no sign of Selina.

It was, however, a beautiful day. Just as bright as yesterday, but cooler, with a good sea running in from the harbour mouth. The pines tossed their spicy heads in the breeze, and small waves slapped cheerfully on the slipways below him. He was filled with pleasure by every prospect. Blue sky, blue sea, *Eclipse* dipping serenely at her moorings, white terrace, red geraniums, all dearly familiar, and yet, this morning, magically fresh. Pearl was sitting on the end of the jetty, consuming a delicious morsel of fish-offal she had found; Frances was back in San Antonio, and Juanita was making him a pot of coffee. He could not remember when he had felt so well, so hopeful or so optimistic. It was as though he had been living for months in the murky gloom of a potential storm, and now the storm was over and the pressure had lifted and he could breathe freely again.

He told himself that he was a heel, that he should be grovelling in a pit of self-hate and remorse, but his sense of physical well-being was too much for his conscience. All this

162

time he had been leaning, with his hands flat, on the wall of the terrace, and now, when he straightened and stood up, he saw that his palms were chalked with white-wash. His automatic reaction was to wipe them clean on his jeans, but all at once his attention was drawn to the convolutions of his own fingerprints, outlined in the white-wash and as delicately drawn as a microscopic chart. A chart of himself, unique to George Dyer, just as the life he had led, and the things he was doing now, were unique.

He was not especially proud of himself. He had, over the years, hurt and offended too many people, and last night, the climax of it all, did not even bear thinking about. But none of this could take away from his present elating sense of identity.

I've grown accustomed to her face.

The record ended and he went inside to turn it off. As he shut the lid of the player he said, "Juanita."

She was spooning coffee into his jug.

"Señor?"

"Juanita, did you know that Pepe, the husband of Maria, had taken the Señorita to the airport yesterday afternoon?"

"*Sí,* Señor," said Juanita, but she was not looking at him.

"Did he tell you that he brought the Señorita back again?"

"*Sí,* Señor. All the village knows."

It was inevitable, and George sighed, but persevered in his interrogation.

"And did Pepe say that the Señorita had lost her passport?"

"He did not know that it was lost. Just that she did not have it."

"But she told the Guardia Civil at the airport?"

"I do not know, Señor." She poured boiling water into the coffee jug.

"Juanita . . ." When she did not turn, he laid his hand on her bare forearm, and her head swung round, and to his amazement he saw that she was laughing at him, her dark eyes bright with amusement. "Juanita . . . the Señorita is not my daughter."

"No, Señor," said Juanita, demurely.

"Don't tell me you already knew."

"Señor," she shrugged, "Pepe did not think that she was behaving like your daughter."

"How was she behaving?"

"She was very unhappy, Señor."

"Juanita, she is not my daughter, but my little cousin."

"Sí, Señor."

"Will you tell Maria? And tell Maria to tell Tomeu, and maybe Tomeu will tell Rosita and Rosita will tell Rudolfo . . ." They were both laughing. "I did not tell a lie, Juanita. But I did not tell the truth either."

"The Señor does not need to worry. If she is a daughter or a cousin . . ." Juanita shrugged enormously as though the question were too trivial for consideration. "But to Cala Fuerte, the Señor is a friend. Nothing else matters."

Such eloquence was foreign to Juanita, and George was so touched he could have kissed her, but he knew that this would have embarrassed them both enormously, so instead he said that he was hungry, and, feeling companionable, he joined her in the kitchen to look in the bread jar and find something that he could smother in butter and apricot jam.

As usual the bread jar was full and had been replenished on top of the old bread. He said, reproachfully, "Juanita, this is very dirty. The bread at the bottom has got a blue beard." And to prove his point, he turned the crock upside down and emptied all the bread out on to the floor. The last mouldy crust fell out, and then the sheet of white paper with which Juanita had lined the bottom of the jar, and finally a slim, dark-blue folder.

It lay on the floor between them, and they stared at each

other in question, each imagining that the other must be responsible.

"What is that thing?"

George picked it up, and turned it over in his hands. "It's a passport. A British passport."

"But who does it belong to?"

"I think, the Señorita."

The idea was to start, not at the beginning of the voyage, but in the middle—the week that *Eclipse* had slid into the harbour at Delos. And then he would go back to the beginning to show, in a series of back-flashes, how the voyage had taken shape, how it had all been planned in the first place. His typing-paper felt thick and smooth and his typewriter was running as sweetly as a well-tuned engine. Selina was still swimming, and Juanita was in her wash-house, beating hell out of George's sheets with her bar of soap, and warbling away at some local love-song, so that when the knock came at the door, he did not hear it.

It was a very discreet knock and scarcely audible above the pounding of his typewriter, and after a little the door was pushed open, and this movement caught George's eye and he looked up, his hands suspended over the typewriter keys.

The man who stood there was young, tall, and very good-looking. He wore a suit, a regular business suit, and a stiff white collar and a tie, and yet he managed to look maddeningly fresh and cool, and he said, "I am sorry to disturb you, but I got no reply to my knocking. Is this the Casa Barco?"

"Yes, it is."

"Then you must be George Dyer."

"Yes, I am. . . ." He stood up.

"My name is Rodney Ackland." He obviously felt that the conversation should not go further without some sort of ritual recognition. He came across the room to shake George's hand. "How do you do?" George thought *Firm grip. Keen, straight eye, thoroughly reliable.* And then, as an unworthy after-thought, *Dead bore.*

"I believe Selina Bruce is staying here?"

"Yes, she is." Rodney looked around in mild question. "She's swimming just now."

"I see. Well, in that case, perhaps I'd better give you some sort of an explanation. I'm Selina's lawyer." George did not comment on this. "And I'm afraid that, indirectly, it was my fault that she made this trip to San Antonio in the first place. It was I who gave her your book, and she saw your photograph and became convinced that you were her father. She spoke to me about it; she told me that she wanted to come and find you, and suggested that I should accompany her, but unfortunately I was forced to make a business trip to Bourne-mouth to see a very important client, and when I returned to London, Selina had gone. By then she'd been away three or four days. So, of course, I caught the first available plane to San Antonio, and . . . well, I think I should take her back." They eyed each other. Rodney said, "Of course, you aren't her father."

"No, I'm not. Her father's dead."

"There is, however, a singular resemblance. Even I can see that."

"Gerry Dawson was a distant cousin of mine."

"What an extraordinary coincidence!"

"Yes," said George. "Extraordinary."

For the first time, Rodney looked a little discomfited. "Mr. Dyer, I have no idea of the circumstances of this . . . rather unconventional visit of Selina's, or even how much she's told you about herself. But she's always had a great desire . . . an obsession, really, about her father. She was brought up by her grandmother, and her childhood was different, to put it mildly. . . ."

"Yes, she told me."

"In that case, as you know the facts, I'm sure we're batting on the same side."

"Yes, I expect we are." He grinned and added, "Purely out of interest, however, what would your reactions have been had I really turned out to be Selina's father?"

"Well . . ." Caught for the moment without words, Rodney floundered. "Well, I . . . er . . ." And then he decided to turn it into a joke, and laughed gamely. "I suppose I should have caught you over the port and nuts, and asked your permission."

"My *permission*?"

"Yes. A bit late, of course, because we're already engaged. We're getting married next month."

George said, "I beg your pardon," and the words themselves were an indication of his state of mind. He had not used the outmoded formality for years, since the Bradderford days of polite parties and Hunt Balls, and had imagined that it was consigned to oblivion. But here it came, back again, jolted out of his subconscious by sheer shock.

"We're already engaged. You surely knew that?"

"No, I didn't know."

"You mean Selina didn't tell you? She is an extraordinary girl."

"Why the hell should she tell me? It's nothing to do with me if she's engaged or not."

"No, but you'd think it would be important. The first thing she'd talk about." George thought, *You conceited clotheshorse.* "But that's beside the point. Now that you're in the picture, I'm sure you'll realise that I should take her back to London, and as quickly as possible."

"Yes, of course."

Rodney eased past him and went out on to the terrace. "What a splendid view! Did you say Selina was swimming? I can't see her."

George joined him. "No, she's, uh, out beyond the yacht.

I'll fetch her for you. . . ." And then he remembered that he couldn't, because she had taken the dinghy. And then he remembered that he could, because he would borrow the boat of Rafael, Tomeu's cousin. "Look . . . can you wait here? Take a seat. Make yourself at home. I won't be long."

"You wouldn't like me to come with you?" Rodney sounded unenthusiastic, and George said, "No, it's all right. The boat's full of fish-scales, and you'd ruin your suit."

"Well, if your sure . . ." and before George's eyes, Rodney pulled a cane chair forward into the sun, and subsided gracefully into it, the picture of the well-bred Englishman abroad.

George dragged the boat of Tomeu's cousin Rafael down the slipway and into the water, swearing with every breath. It was long and heavy and awkward to handle, and there was only one oar so he had to scull, which he did inexpertly, and this in itself was infuriating, because Rodney Ackland, with his smooth bland face and his smooth bland voice and his uncreased charcoal-grey suit was watching him from the terrace of the Casa Barco. He made his way, rocking and sweating and swearing, across the water to where *Eclipse* lay, but when he called Selina's name there was no reply.

With some difficulty he manoeuvred his unwieldly craft around *Eclipse*'s stern mooring-rope, and immediately spied Selina, perched like a mermaid on one of the rocks on the far shore. She had climbed up the bathing-steps of one of the little wedding-cake villas that nestled in the pine trees and she sat with her arms wrapped around her knees and her hair lay close and wet to her neck like the fur of a seal. Rafael's boat slid beneath *Eclipse*'s port beam. George shipped the heavy oar, and stood, cupping his hands to call her again.

"*Selina!*" It came out as an infuriated yell, and she looked up at once. "Come on in, I want to talk to you."

After only a second's hesitation, she stood up and came down the white steps, and let herself into the water and swam back towards him. When she reached the boat, the gunwales were too high for her to climb over, so he had to put his hands under her shoulders and lift her in, wet and dripping as a freshly caught fish. They sat on the two thwarts, facing each other, and she said, "I am sorry. Did you want the dinghy?"

It occurred to him that any other woman would have demanded, before another word was spoken, an apology for his behaviour of the night before. But Selina was not any other woman.

"I hope you didn't mind my taking it . . ."

"No of course not."

"You were asleep when I came down. I had to let Juanita in." He watched her speak, not hearing what she said, trying to reconcile himself to the shattering knowledge that she was going to marry Rodney Ackland, had been engaged all the time, had never told George.

". . . and is your friend all right? She wasn't too angry, I hope."

"My friend? Oh, Frances. I don't know if she's angry or not. She drove back to San Antonio last night. Anyway, it wasn't your fault. She'll simmer down and it'll be all forgotten."

"I shouldn't have come back to the Casa Barco, I do see that now, but . . ."

He could bear it no longer. "Selina."

She frowned. "Is something wrong?"

"Listen. There's someone waiting for you at the Casa Barco. He's come to take you back to London. Rodney Ackland."

She seemed to freeze to stillness. Her lips said "Rodney" but no sound came out.

"He flew from London last night. He got back from Bournemouth and realised that you'd come to San Antonio on your own, so he caught the first available flight. I told him that

I wasn't your father, and I must say, he didn't seem particularly surprised. But he does want to talk to you."

The breeze blew coolly and Selina shivered. He saw the thin gold chain, disappearing into the top of the little bikini he had bought her, but now he knew that it was not a Confirmation cross that hung there. He reached out and took hold of the chain and lifted it free, and the sapphire and diamonds of Rodney Ackland's engagement ring swung and spun before his eyes, sharp arrows of sunlight darting from every facet.

"Selina. Why did you never tell me?"

Her eyes at that moment seemed almost as blue as the sapphire that he dangled beneath her chin. "I don't know."

"You are engaged to Rodney?" She nodded. "You're going to marry him next month." She nodded again. "But why does it all have to be so secret?"

"It isn't secret. I told Rodney about you. I told him I thought George Dyer was my father. And I wanted him to come with me and find you. But he couldn't. He had business to see to in Bournemouth, and he never thought I'd come alone. He said that if you were my father, then you'd be embarrassed by my sudden appearance. And if you weren't my father, then it was a wild goose chase anyway. He didn't seem to understand how important it was; to have roots and a family, and really belong to somebody."

"Have you known him a long time?"

"Since I was a little girl. His firm has always looked after my grandmother's affairs. She liked him very much, and I know she hoped I would marry him."

"And now you're going to."

"Yes. I usually ended up by doing what she wanted." George's dark eyes were suddenly compassionate and Selina could not bear him to be sorry for her. "We're moving out of Queen's Gate. We've found a lovely flat in a new block. I wish you could see it. It's full of sunshine and it's got a wonderful view. Agnes is going to come and live with us. I've even bought my wedding-dress. It's white, and very long. With a train."

"But you wear your engagement ring hidden away, not even on a finger."

"I thought you were my father. I wanted to meet you, for the first time, just as myself. Not belonging to any other person, or any other way of life."

"Are you in love with him?"

"I asked *you* that question yesterday, and you wouldn't reply."

"That was different. We were talking about my past and this is your future."

"Yes, I know. That's what makes it so important."

He did not reply to this. Now Selina put up her hands to the back of her neck and unfastened the gold chain. The ring slipped free and she caught it and put it back on her finger and then re-fastened the chain once more about her neck. All these actions were deliberate and entirely composed. She said, "I shouldn't keep Rodney waiting."

"No, of course not. Take the dinghy back, and I'll follow on in this great crate of Rafael's. But don't sneak off without saying good-bye."

"I'd never do that. You know I'd never do that."

After a little, Rodney had found it too hot to wait on the terrace. He could have taken off his jacket, but he was wearing braces, and there seemed something almost indecent in sitting about in braces, so he got out of the cane chair and went into the cool of the house. He was prowling to and fro, trying to make head or tail of its unconventional design, when Selina, unnoticed and unheard, came up the steps of the terrace, and said his name.

Stopped short in his prowlings, Rodney swung round. She stood in the open doorway and he stared in disbelief. He could not believe that in such a short time one person could have altered so much. He had always thought of her as a monotone person, fawn skin and fawn hair, only relieved by the bright blue, Siamese-cat eyes. But now she was very brown and her hair, still wet from swimming, was bleached in streaks by the sunshine. She wore a bikini which to Rodney's eyes seemed one step short of sheer bad taste, and as she stood there, regarding him, the large white cat which had been sunning itself on the terrace came to wrap itself affectionately around her bare ankles.

The moment was fraught with a strange embarrassment. Then Selina said, "Hello, Rodney. This is a surprise." She tried to put a lift in her voice but it fell sadly flat on the last syllable.

"Yes," said Rodney, "I thought it would be." It was not easy to believe that he had just made the journey from London, had sat up all night in his clothes, had walked from the village down the stony, dusty road to the Casa Barco. Admittedly, his shoes were lightly veiled in white, but otherwise he looked as immaculate as he did at home. He came to give her a kiss, his hands on her shoulders, and he held her off to raise mildly disapproving eyebrows at her bikini. "What's this you're wearing?"

She shrugged, "It's all I have to swim in." There was an old towel coat of George's draped over the washing-line, and she went to collect it, and put it on. The towel was hard and dry with salt and sun and smelt of George. She wrapped it tightly about her, and in some inexplicable way it comforted her, and bolstered her courage.

He said, "You were naughty to come out without letting me know. I might have been out of my mind with worry."

"I knew you were in Bournemouth."

"I called the flat as soon as I got back to London and Agnes told me where you were." He added, "I came straight out, of course, on the first available flight."

"That was very kind of you, Rodney."

"How do you feel about coming home?"

172

"I would have been back before, only I had all my money stolen at the airport, and I couldn't buy a return ticket."

"You surely could have let me know; I'd have cabled you some by return."

"I . . . I didn't want to bother you. And," she added on a burst of honesty, "I thought you'd just say 'I told you so.' Because you were right and I was wrong, and George Dyer wasn't my father . . . isn't my father . . ."

"No, I rather gathered that."

"But you do see that I had to find out?" It was a plea for sympathy, but Rodney misunderstood her.

"I'm afraid I still feel it would have been better had you let me do the finding out for you."

"But I asked you to come with me. I wanted you to come, but you wouldn't."

"Not wouldn't. Couldn't. You know that."

"You could have put off Mrs. What's-her-name."

"Selina!" He was deeply shocked, and realised then, perhaps for the first time, that the changes in her were not merely physical, but deeper and far more subtle.

She took a deep breath.

"Anyway," she said, "I don't regret any of it. I'm glad I came, even if George isn't my father. And if I were asked, I'd do it all over again."

It was an invitation to a stand-up battle, but before Rodney could think up any reply, they were joined by George Dyer himself, who came up the terrace steps, gathered Pearl into his arms, and chipped cheerfully into the conversation.

"Well, now, isn't this nice? You've found each other again. How about a drink to cool us all down?"

"I won't have a drink, thank you," said Rodney stiffly.

"Cigarette, then?"

"No, not just now." He cleared his throat. "I've been telling Selina that I think it would be a good idea if we were to

173

return to London as soon as possible. My taxi's waiting now at the Cala Fuerte Hotel; we can go straight back to the airport."

"Good organisation," said George.

Rodney glanced at him swiftly to see if George was laughing at him, but the dark eyes were very solemn. Not entirely reassured he turned back to Selina. "Perhaps you should pack. Where have you been staying?"

There was a long silence. Rodney looked at Selina. Selina looked at George and then back to Rodney. George, with great nonchalance, stroked Pearl.

Selina said, "Here."

Rodney seemed to blanch visibly. "*Here?*"

"Yes. Here. At the Casa Barco."

"*Sleeping* here?"

"There wasn't anywhere else to go. . . ."

She shivered slightly and George knew that she was nervous. Rodney, however, did not seem aware of this, for when he spoke it was in tones of ice.

"Wasn't that just the *slightest* bit unconventional?"

Abruptly, George tipped Pearl into a handy chair and joined in the discussion. "I don't think so. After all, let's not forget, Selina is a cousin of mine."

"And let's not forget how distant. Besides, that is scarcely the point."

"Then what is the point?"

"Well, Selina turned up here, uninvited, unannounced, a complete stranger to you, and you let her *stay;* living in this house—practically, as far as I can see, sleeping in the same room. I quite appreciate that you don't necessarily have to consider your own reputation, but for Selina's sake you could surely have made some other arrangement."

"Perhaps we didn't want to," said George.

Rodney lost his temper. "I'm sorry, Mr. Dyer, but we obviously don't speak the same language. I find your attitude insufferable."

174

"I am sorry."

"Do you always have such scant regard for the normal, decent rules of behaviour?"

"Yes, always. And they aren't my rules."

For a moment Rodney toyed with the thought of knocking him down, but then decided that George was beyond contempt and only fit to be ignored. He turned to Selina.

"Selina . . ." She seemed to start visibly. "I'm sorry about this, but I give you the benefit of believing that it was none of it your fault. I'm quite prepared to forget about it all, but we must make sure that no whisper of what has happened ever reaches London."

Selina regarded him gravely. His face was smooth and well-shaved. He didn't seem to have any lines on it at all, and it was impossible to imagine him growing old, experienced and pleasantly worn-looking. He would be like this when he was eighty, as impersonal and unruffled as a newly-laundered shirt.

She said, "Why, Rodney?"

"I . . . I wouldn't like Mr. Arthurstone to hear of it."

It was such a ridiculous reply that she wanted to laugh. Mr. Arthurstone, with his arthritic knees, who was going to give her away . . . what on earth had it got to do with Mr. Arthurstone? "And now"—Rodney glanced at his watch— "there's no more time to waste. Get on some clothes and we'll get going."

George was lighting himself a cigarette as Rodney said this. Now he shook out the match, took the cigarette out of his mouth and said, "She can't come to London with you. She's lost her passport."

"She's . . . *what?*"

"Lost her passport. It happened yesterday. Most extraordinary."

"Is this true, Selina?"

"Oh. I . . . well, yes . . ."

George bulldozed her into silence. "Of course it's true.

My dear Mr. Ackland, you can have no idea what it's like out here. They'd steal the gold out of your teeth if they could lay their hands on it."

"But your *passport*. Selina, do you realise how serious this is?"

"Well . . . I . . ." Selina floundered.

"Have you informed the British Consul?"

"No," said George, taking charge once more, "but she told the Guardia Civil at the airport, and very understanding and helpful they were, too."

"It amazes me that they didn't throw her straight into jail."

"I was pretty amazed too, but of course it's wonderful what a pretty smile can do, even in Spain."

"But what steps are we going to take?"

"Well, now you ask me, I would suggest that you go and get into that taxi and go back to London, and leave Selina here with me . . . No," he halted Rodney's infuriated protests, "I really think this is the best plan. You can possibly pull some strings at your end and between us we ought to be able to keep her out of prison. And don't worry too much about the conventions, old boy. After all, I'm probably Selina's nearest relative, and I'm perfectly prepared to take responsibility for her. . . ."

"Responsibility? You?" He made a final appeal to Selina. "Surely you don't *want* to stay here?" Rodney nearly exploded at the thought.

"Well . . ." Her very hesitation was enough to convince him.

"You amaze me! Your selfishness amazes me! You don't seem to realise that it isn't just your good name. I have a certain reputation to keep up as well, and I find your attitude incredible! What Mr. Arthurstone will have to say, I dread to think."

"But you'll be able to explain to Mr. Arthurstone, Rodney.

I'm sure you'll be able to explain. And I think . . . while your explaining, you'd better tell him that he won't have to give me away after all. I really am awfully sorry, but I'm sure, in a way, it's a relief to you. After all, you wouldn't want to be saddled with me, not after what's happened. And . . . here's your ring. . . ."

She held it out in her palm, the winking diamonds and the deep blue sapphire that he had imagined would bind her to him for ever. He longed to be able to make the grand gesture to take the ring, and fling it out over the terrace wall and into the sea beyond, but it had cost him a great deal of money, so he swallowed his pride and took it back.

"I am sorry, Rodney."

It seemed most dignified to maintain a manly silence. Rodney turned on his heel and made for the door, but George was there first, holding it open for him. "A shame you've had such an unproductive visit. You should come to Cala Fuerte later on in the year when there's more going on. I'm sure you'd enjoy the water-skiing and the aqua-lunging and the spear-fishing. It was good of you to come."

"Please don't imagine, Mr. Dyer, that I or my partners will let you get away with this."

"I don't imagine so for a moment. I'm sure Mr. Arthurstone will have some bright ideas up his sleeve, and in due course I shall be on the receiving end of a stiff letter. Sure I can't run you to the village?"

"Thank you, I prefer to walk."

"Oh well, *chacun à son gout.* It's been splendid meeting you. Good-bye."

But Rodney did not reply, merely marched in silent fury from the house. George saw him safely on his way up the hill, and then closed the door behind him.

He turned. Selina stood, still in the middle of the room where Rodney had left her. She looked as if she were expecting another violent scene, but he only said, in his most reasonable of tones, "You ought to get your head examined, thinking you'd ever marry a man like that. You'd spend half your time changing for dinner, and the other half looking up all those long words in the dictionary. And who's Mr. Arthurstone, anyway?"

"He's the senior partner of the firm Rodney works for. He's very old and he's got arthritis in his knees."

"And he was going to give you away?"

"There wasn't anyone else."

It was a forlorn admission. George said, "Are you talking about Mr. Arthurstone, or are you talking about Rodney?"

"Both, I suppose."

"Perhaps," said George gently, "perhaps you were suffering from a bad attack of father-fixation."

"Yes. Perhaps I was."

"And now?"

"Not any more."

She shivered again, and he smiled. "You know, Selina, I would never have believed it possible how much you can learn about another person in such a ridiculously short time. For instance, I know that when you lie, which is sadly frequent, your eyes get so wide and so big that the blue bits are almost entirely surrounded by white. Like islands. And when you're trying not to laugh at some outrageous thing I've said, you turn down the corners of your mouth and somehow conjure up a very unexpected dimple. And when you're nervous you shiver. You're nervous now."

"I'm not nervous. I'm cold from swimming."

"Then go and put some clothes on."

"But I must tell you something first. . . ."

"It can keep. Run along and get dressed."

He went out on to the terrace to wait for her. He lit a cigarette and the sun was hot on his shoulders, burning through the thin cotton of his shirt. Rodney Ackland had gone, away from the Casa Barco, out of Selina's life. Just as Jenny had gone, her ghost laid for ever, the unhappy affair exorcised for ever by the simple act of telling Selina about her. Jenny and Rodney were both in the past, and the present felt gay and good, and the future as hopeful and as filled with pleasant surprises as a Christmas package.

Below him, in the garden, Juanita was pegging out sheets, still singing happily to herself and apparently unaware of the drama that had taken place while she tackled the morning laundry. He was filled with a sudden surge of affection for her. No one knew better than himself that George's own personal road to hell had always been paved with good intentions, but now he promised himself that when the new book was published he would give her, not merely a presentation copy to sit on a lace doily, but something more. Something that she wanted badly, that she would never be able to buy for herself. A silk dress, or a jewel, or a fine new gas stove.

Selina's footstep behind him made him turn. She wore a sleeveless linen dress the colour of apricots, and sandals with little heels that made her almost as tall as he, and it astounded him that it had taken so long to realise that she was beautiful. He said, "This is the first time I've seen you properly dressed. I'm glad you got your luggage back."

Selina took a keep breath. She said, "George, I have to talk to you."

"What about?"

"My passport."

"What about your passport?"

"Well. You see. It isn't lost at all."

He started, and frowned in enormous surprise. "It *isn't*?"

"No. You see . . . well, yesterday afternoon, before I went off with Pepe . . . I hid it."

"Selina." He sounded deeply shocked. "Why did you do a dreadful thing like that?"

"I know it was dreadful, but I didn't want to go. I didn't

179

want to leave you with Mrs. Dongen. I knew she didn't want you to write that second book. She wanted you to go off to Australia or the Gobi desert or somewhere. With her. So when I went to the kitchen to get the soda water out of the refrigerator, I . . ." she swallowed. "I hid my passport in the bread jar."

"What an extraordinary thing to do!"

"Yes, I know. But I was only thinking of you, and what I'm trying to say is that there's no reason now why I shouldn't go back to London with Rodney. I mean, I shan't get married to him, of course. I see how stupid I was even to imagine that I could. But I can't stay here indefinitely." Her voice began to tail away. George was being absolutely no help at all. "You do see that, don't you?"

"Well, of course I do." He assumed the expression of a man who would go to any lengths to see fair play. "And we must do the right thing."

"Yes . . . yes; that's what I thought."

"Well," he went on bracingly, glancing at his watch, "if you're going with Rodney, you'd better get your skates on, otherwise he'll be in his taxi and away before you've even reached the Cala Fuerte Hotel. . . ."

And before her incredulous eyes, he stood up, dusted the whitewash from the seat of his jeans, and the next moment was back at his typewriter, working away as though his life depended upon it.

It was not exactly the reaction Selina had hoped for. She waited for some sort of reprieve, but none came, and so, trying to swallow the lump in her throat and blink away a ridiculous burning suspicion of tears, she went to the kitchen, and took out the bread jar and emptied it, loaf by loaf on to the counter, eventually removing the sheet of paper under which she had slipped her passport.

It was not there. Tears, disappointment, everything was drowned in a wave of sheer panic. Her passport was really lost.

"George!" He was typing so hard that he did not hear her. "George, I've . . . *I've lost my passport.*"

He stopped typing and raised polite eyebrows. "Again?"

"It's not here! I put it at the very bottom, and it's not here! I've lost it!"

"Good lord!" said George.

"What could have happened?" Her voice rose to a wail. "Could Juanita have found it? Or perhaps she cleaned out the jar and she's burned it. Or thrown it away! Perhaps it's been stolen. Oh, what will happen to me?"

"I don't like to imagine. . . ."

"I wish I'd never put it there in the first place!"

"You've been hoist with your own petard," said George in sanctimonious tones, and returned to his typing.

Suspicion nudged at Selina at last, and she frowned. Surely he was behaving in an unnaturally calm fashion? And there had been a gleam in his dark eyes that she had learned not to trust. Had he found the passport? Had he found it, and hidden it, and never told her? Leaving the empty bread jar, she moved around the room, casually searching for clues, lifting the corner of the magazine, peering behind a cushion, as though she were playing a game of Hunt the Thimble.

She finished up behind him. He wore his worn, salt-stained jeans, and the back pocket on the right hip looked curiously square and stiff, as though it contained a small book, or a large card. . . . He was still typing full blast, but, when Selina reached out her hand to investigate the pocket, his own hand came round and slapped it away.

The panic was over. She laughed, in relief; in happiness; in love. She put her arms around his neck and nearly strangled him in her embrace and she said, "You've got it! You found it! You had it all the time, you brute!"

"Do you want it back?"

"Not unless you want me to go to London with Rodney."

"I don't," said George.

181

She kissed him, rubbing her own soft cheek against his rough, bristly one, and it was not smooth and scented with after-shave, but creased and sun-browned and netted with lines, as worn and familiar as one of his own rough-dried cotton work shirts. She said, "I don't want to go either." He had written a full page of typescript. Selina rested her chin on the top of his head and said, "What are you writing?"

"A synopsis."

"For the new book? What's it about?"

"The cruise to the Aegean."

"What's it going to be called?"

"I haven't the faintest idea, but I'll dedicate it to you."

"Is it going to be good?"

"I hope so. But in fact, I've already got an idea for a third book. Fiction this time. . . ." He took her hand, and pulled her around so that she was sitting on the edge of his desk, facing him. "I thought it could be about this chap, living in some quiet little spot, not doing a living soul a mite of harm, minding his own business. And then, along comes this tramp of a girl. She has an obsession about him. Won't leave him alone. Alienates all his friends, spends all his money, drives him to drink. He becomes a derelict, a social outcast."

"What happens in the end?"

"He marries her, of course. She tricks him into it. There's no escape. It's tragic."

"It doesn't sound tragic to me."

"Well, it ought to."

"George, are you, by any chance, asking me to marry you?"

"I suppose, in my warped, twisted way, I am; I'm sorry about last night. And I do love you."

"I know you do." She leaned forward to kiss his mouth. "I'm glad you do." She kissed him again, and he pushed his typewriter out of the way, and stood up to gather her into his arms. Later, Selina said, "We'll have to let Agnes know."

"She won't come out here and try to throw a spanner in the works?"

"Of course not. She'll love you."

"We'll have to send her a cable. From San Antonio. This afternoon, if it's to get to her before Rodney Ackland does. And while we're in town, we'll go and pay our respects to the English padre and find out what the delay is. And we'll ask Rudolfo to be my best man. . . ."

"I wish I could have Juanita as a bridesmaid."

Juanita. They had forgotten Juanita. Now, still laughing, hand in hand, they went out to find her, to lean over the wall of the terrace and call her name. But Juanita was not as simple as she sometimes appeared. Her peasant instincts seldom let her down, and already she was on her way up from the garden, erect as ever and beaming with pleasure, and with her arms outstretched as though to embrace them both.